AFTER THE GOLD RUSH

**Third Flatiron Anthologies
Volume 11, Book 31, Summer/Fall 2022**

**Edited by Juliana Rew
Cover Art by Keely Rew**

After the Gold Rush
Third Flatiron Anthologies
Volume 11, Summer/Fall 2022

Published by Third Flatiron Publishing
Juliana Rew, Editor and Publisher

License Notes

www.thirdflatiron.com

Contents

*****~~~~~*****

10

Editor's Note

As Third Flatiron celebrates 10 years, we welcome you to our 32nd outing. We're honored that over the years, we've featured the work of more than 350 authors, and have podcasted more than 50 of their stories. We're also proud of the mix of Colorado and international writers.

This all-original SFFH anthology has the theme, "After the Gold Rush." We asked contributors to explore themes related to complications of booms and bubbles, including effects of accelerated culture; ecological consequences caused by human over-expansion, such as climate disasters; and economics (for example, resources and commodities).

We are especially grateful to Wulf Moon, who leads his "Super Secrets" workshop that he began in the Writers of the Future Forum. He encouraged writers to submit to our latest call, and by our count, seven "Wulf Pack" authors of the twenty-one in this anthology are new to our pages.

So, what have we got in store for you this time?

We might get more than we bargained for as the latest gadgets accelerate and overtake us. We lead off with

James Tager's "Past the Projections," a creative—and creepy—story in which AI robotics come to life in virtual reality. The intelligent drone "bees" in Tim Borella's "To Vanquish Other Blooms" repeat the adage, *it's not nice to fool Mother Nature.*

We offer a number of instructive "what-if" stories about corporations that corner valuable resources, such as sunlight and real estate. With ingenuity and valor, ordinary people might still find ways to come out on top. Such a story is Robert Bagnall's "Sunrunner," an affecting story, about a rebel sunlight thief. We cheer Julie Biegner's teens as they try to take down the VR monopoly that's become a fascist state in her story, "Amphibios." Also, check out "Reassessed Value," by David Hankins, about a farmer who discovers a corporate loophole to save his land.

After climate change: Are we hearing the strains of the orchestra playing "Nearer, My God, to Thee?" In "Moving On," by Andrew Wright, Cape Cod is now an island, and it's Harry's job to check on houses and gardens before another storm arrives.

A gold rush theme means there's always room for a weird western, right? On the boomtown planet of Proxima B, when a samurai lawman is called to investigate a death, he discovers an ancient Mexican cult, in "Showdown at Sueño Hueco" by Wulf Moon.

"Earth's Last Immortals," by Erin Cullen, is the story of a future where life-extension technology has made it possible for humans to technically become immortal, but at what cost?

In a world where the world has retreated into virtual reality, a man searches for people who will return to "real" reality. "Facing Reality" by Yelena Crane.

In "Last Light in the Dark" by Shannon Fox, an actor on a far-future planet decides a change of pace is in order when his family's line of work starts to deviate from his personal values. While other stories about the after-effects of gold rush "bubbles" are usually sad, we find a nugget of hope.

It's hot. Damn hot. In Edward Barnfield's, story, "Live from the Troll Factory," hackers toil away in a post-internet apocalyptic sweatshop. It reminded us a bit of Margaret Atwood's *Oryx and Crake*—only with computers.

Not all is gloom and doom, however.

There's evidence there was once a lot of water on the moon, so there may be a future call for explorers to find hidden reservoirs. Enjoy David Cleden's "Down on the Klondike," as a young man buys a stake on the Moon with his mother's credit card and runs into disaster almost immediately. In "The Front of the Pack," Lauren C. Teffeau's satirical story, this captured prisoner is not an arms dealer, he offers a scarce service—he's a regulation evasion provider.

Bon Voyage: In "Last Bite at the Klondike," by Liam Hogan, we meet an asteroid miner who opts to test the "interstellar progress paradox" rather than return to Earth

We loved the movie, "CODA" (Children of Deaf Adults). If humans ever make first contact, it'll be important to find what we have in common. "All Our Signs Align" by Eve Morton, introduces a translator who teaches aliens American Sign Language (ASL).

"Unwinding the Clock" by Brandon Case, tells the satirical story of a grandma hacker who codes a scam app and sends the proceeds to a deserving recipient

Like William Wallace said in "Braveheart:" Freeeedom!! "The Last of the Gen Xers" by Angelique Fawns, is the story of a guy with an outlawed gas-guzzling Cadillac.

As usual, we conclude with our flash humor section, "Grins & Gurgles," with a "Currency Change

Announcement" by Elizabeth Davis; "Amore for Life" by Cray Dimensional; "Genie in a PET Bottle" by Daniel M. Cojocaru; and "Goldberry" by Tom Easton and Jeff Hecht. We hope you are prepared for *After the Gold Rush.*

Enjoy,
Juliana Rew
July 2022

*****~~~~*****

Past the Projections

by James Tager

She was flickering again. Damn it. Steven focused on pouring his drink. Behind him, she was pleading. "We should run away together, forget about this war. Steven, look at me!"

Steven turned around and looked straight at her. Five foot seven, red dress, black hair. The love of his life. Anastasia. Ana, for short. He had paid extra to be able to personalize her name. He had paid extra for a lot of personalization options, including extra to guarantee the end of this god-damn flickering. Money wasted, apparently.

Even as he watched, Ana's body winked out, winked back into existing, appearing unnaturally stretched, the colors washed. "Following General Anchorage's orders will get you killed, Steven. You know that." Her voice came out unnaturally high, as if the room had been tinged with helium. Steven scowled. The wonders of technology.

He remembered the time when he was still impressed with how the technology had worked. The website for Greater Life Technologies (tagline: Socially Isolated, but Never Alone) had explained to him how GLT technicians, following social distancing protocol, would install a generator in his basement along with a series of

11

projectors and speakers throughout his house. The result, the website explained, would be a complex illusion, an ever-changing movie set recreated in his house. The technology was cutting edge, not only freeing the actors from the screen but imbuing them with a sense of life and spontaneity as they interacted with the objects in Steven's own home.

Steven sighed. "Have a drink, doll. You're getting yourself all worked up over nothing." He tried to deliver the line the way Bogart would, with a half-sneer and a distracted mien. But he found it hard to play along with the scenario, to suspend his disbelief, when before his eyes Ana winked in and out.

"*Nothing!* You're going off on a suicide mission!" Now the volume was fluctuating, dropping her voice down to a whisper before ratcheting it up to a scream.

Steven shook his head in renewed irritation. "GLT, pause Casablanca simulation." There was a low beep, and Ana froze before him. Steven stared at her as he drank. She was frozen in mid-word. The light glinted off of her diamond necklace. Her hair was perfectly coiffed, her dark eyes inviting, her lips cherry-red.

A perfect illusion. Spoiled by yet another technical difficulty. The third one this past year. And with GLT now forced out of business, there was no technician he could call.

Steven thought. If both the audio and the video projection were malfunctioning, it had to be a problem with the projector. Nothing for it, but to go down to the storage room and reboot. Not for the first time, he cursed the company who sold him this damn machine, and the overzealous regulators that had shut the company down.

Cursed himself, for preferring the fantasy of GLT's simulations to his own shitty, isolated life.

Steven finished his drink, then poured himself another. He drank it quickly, grimacing as the alcohol burned its way down. To the generator, then.

Past the Projections

The storage room was hidden away in a basement annex. Behind a nondescript wooden door, the room was further separated from the rest of the house by a heavy iron grate secured with a thick padlock. Steven jingled his keys in one hand, the other holding the door open, peering past the grate to the other end of the long room. There, the generator hummed lowly, its blinking white lights the only illumination in the otherwise black room.

Steeling himself, Steven unlocked the grate, stepped through, and brought the padlock around to lock it again. He hated the feeling of locking himself in, had to fight back an irrational moment of panic, the fleeting fear that he would lose the keys and be trapped in the storage room forever. But the moment passed. Steven had learned, on a previous trip, the need to make sure that he was the only thing that entered or exited the storage room. Had learned the hard way.

It was only a couple hundred feet to the generator. Steven forced himself to walk slowly, not to run. He reminded himself that there was nothing to be afraid of.

The first few steps, the only sound was the soles of his shoes slapping against the concrete floor. After the first few steps, however, Steven began to hear the soft scuffles of other feet than his, the squeaks of slow movements, the low rhythm of breaths. Despite himself, he peered quickly into the dark around him, his eyes slowly adjusting to the lack of light.

At first, he caught only flashes, hard to make out without any light. The tip of an unpolished shoe. The hem of a dress. An upturned palm, ashen and gray in the dark. A gray face, gazing unblinkingly back at him. As he continued to walk, he saw more. More faces, more pale limbs, more outstretched hands.

He hadn't made it halfway across the room when they started to walk towards him. He began to walk faster, his heart tightening within his chest.

13

He was almost at the generator when a voice called out to him, "Hello?" His eyes widened, his breath caught in his throat. He forced himself to remain calm, to keep walking. They weren't supposed to talk, he reminded himself, his mind scrabbling for answers. Once they came down to the storage room, they weren't supposed to be able to talk. Just a few more steps, to the generator.

The storage room was large. It had needed to be, to hold everything.

Bathed in the pale white light of the generator, Steven could see them now. The gray figures, the cast-off projections, the actors and actresses who had already taken their curtain calls. The technology gave these recordings enough life to break from their original portrayals and create unique performances, a tiny spark of individuality and whimsy. So when the movie was done, when the projection ended, they remained. Here, near the generator that gave them life.

They weren't really alive, of course, Steven reminded himself. Not like a human being is alive. They were more like a motion detector that had laid dormant, like robots awaiting commands. That was why, when Steven came down to the storage room, they reacted to his presence. They weren't really alive.

"Hello?" Another voice, from the crowd of gray beings that pressed closer to him. A different voice. Steven frowned, his hand resting against the shell of the generator. They weren't supposed to talk.

He looked out at the crowd of faces staring back at him, trying to find the source of the voice. Amongst the dozens of faces—bit parts, minor figures in the plays that increasingly took up the majority of his life—he recognized several major characters. There was Albert, an older man impeccably dressed in a black suit. Next to him was Jeffords, the wise-cracking sidekick, always ready with a quip or a smart remark. Down here, however,

Jeffords was silent. His eyes, normally sparkling with mischief, lay flat and lifeless.

Behind them, hunched down next to a concrete pillar, was Julius, who often played the villain, and whose customary sardonic smirk seemed grim when set against the harsh shadows of this windowless room. Julius would be in an upcoming scene in his Casablanca simulation, Steven knew. He would be summoned upstairs, would appear in a shower of light.

Anastasia, conversely, would return back to the storage room once her scene was finished. She was Steven's favorite. Nowadays, he only picked movies that were love stories, so he could spend more time with her. He'd stared at her face so often, had felt his heart swell with so much tenderness towards her. He'd seen her laugh, seen her cry. But only in color. Never in gray. He only ever came down here when she was still frozen upstairs.

Steven swept his gaze further down, near his own feet. A small child stood in front of him, clad in an ornate dress. He barely recognized her, could not remember the last simulation she had been in or even what he had named her. He remembered that the girl's dress was usually pink, or purple. Now, like everything else in the storage room, even the skin and the lips of the projections, it had washed out into gray.

The girl lifted her arms out to him. She was so young. "Hello?" she asked. Then, "Please?" She lifted her arms higher, almost touching him.

Steven slammed his hand down on the re-start button for the generator. The room was plunged into darkness, replaced a moment later by a flashing red as the generator began to reboot. In the crimson light, the pale projections seemed to press closer against Steven, their eyes seeming more needy.

He had done what he came here to do. Steven pressed past them, forced himself through the mass of shoulders and hands and beseeching looks, heading back to the locked door. He moved quickly, told himself not to turn around. He heard the march of heavy footfalls behind him, the occasional voice. "Hello?" "Please?"

They weren't supposed to talk. Never in the storage room. They were just supposed to sit silently until it was their turn.

He heard a voice say a third word, "Wait?" That was when he broke into a run.

He grabbed at the keys in his pockets as he ran, brought them out, held them in front of him like a cross against evil, or a lifeline. He reached the lock, fitted the key inside, and turned. Throwing off the padlock, he hauled the door open, then allowed himself a quick look around.

They had stopped, a few feet behind him, and stood, silent, motionless, simply staring at him. Rows of them, men and women. Grandfathers from children's stories, love-tossed couples whose romances were always secondary to his own, dirt-smudged orphans, soldiers and detectives and vaudevillians, tough guys and femme fatales, reunited family members, mercenaries and mentors, villains and sidekicks, those who had been crushed by life and those whose stories warmed the heart. His personal, daily, troupe of actors-on-call. The cast of characters who formed a parade at which he was always the head.

His life. A group of people more real to him than the co-workers at the job he had quit, than the women he once knew but never loved, than the family that had given up on him, than the friends he had alienated, than the smiling salesman at GLT who had promised him the world in three easy payments. All there, all gray, all silent. And in the front, the girl whose character he could not remember, with wide eyes, in a once-pink dress.

16

Past the Projections

Steven opened the grate, its harsh screech the only sound. He stepped outside, closed it, slammed the padlock into place. Only then did he let out a breath.

"Wait, please." The child stopped at the other side of the grate. Her hands clutched weakly at the bars. Now framed by the light outside, the child looked frail. Frail, and so small, so young. Steven hesitated, the key still in the lock. "Please," the child whispered, softer now, and softer. Her lips continued to move, but Steven could no longer hear her. He swayed closer to catch the words.

The child's hand snapped out, reaching for his throat. Steven threw himself back, felt the child's nails rend against his skin, felt them draw blood. He fell, hands raised to protect his neck, on the ground. Another moment was spent in shock and fear as the child's hateful eyes burned hungry holes into his own. And then they both went for the key.

Steven got there first. The child's nails sunk into his hand as he withdrew it from the lock. Her nails, had they always been that long? He tried to remember. He hadn't been in the storage room for such a long time. He stood now, inches from the child's reach, and looked again. Had her proportions always been so strange? Had the pupils of her eyes always been so dark?

The child pressed her face against the grate. Her hands clutched at the bars, wretched at them with a savage anger. "Let us out," she hissed through gritted teeth, her strange, gray, teeth. "Let us out, let us out, let us out."

Steven slammed the door shut. His unbloodied hand massaged at his throat absently, his eyes still staring at the door. He could hear the frenzied beating of his own heart, felt the slow trickle of blood falling from his hand and from his neck.

Steven took a breath to steady himself, turning away slowly. It was only as he began to calm down, as his heartbeat slowed, that he realized he could still hear sounds from beyond the door, the words faint to hear, blending together into a strange chant.

"Let us out let us out let us out *let us out.* . .

Steven ran back upstairs and slammed the door to the basement closed. Locked it. Held his breath. Listened.

After a while, he convinced himself that he could no longer hear anything. He took out his cellphone from his front pocket, held it in his hand. Wished there was someone he could call. The technical helpline for Greater Life Technologies, for instance. But that had been shut down, after the company was legislated out of existence. He could call the police, tell them that he wanted to turn in his GLT system. The amnesty period for GLT users was over, he knew, but maybe they'd only slap him with a fine. He could call a lawyer, discuss his legal options.

Steven put his phone back in his pocket. He wanted another drink. He walked back to his living room, back to the bar, his strides lengthening as he put more room between himself and the basement entrance. "GLT, resume Casablanca simulation," he commanded.

Anastasia resumed talking. "I love you too damn much, Steven, to see you throw your life away!"

She had stopped flickering, Steven noted. And her voice sounded fine. He grabbed the bottle of whiskey, poured a generous helping into his glass. Turned to look at her. She was beautiful, alright. And he was her hero. In the simulation, he was everyone's hero.

For a second, he imagined Anastasia down in the basement, gray and lifeless and abandoned. The image morphed slowly in his mind, Anastasia's mouth twisting with hatred, her eyes darkening, her hands lengthening into. . . claws . . .

Steven took a large gulp and shook the thought away. Or tried to, anyway. He could feel the image retreating to the corners of his mind, hidden but not absent. Like the others. Out of sight, but always there. Isolated, but never alone.

18

He considered his next line. In the simulation, he could say anything; the characters would react organically, would work his responses into the script. He closed his eyes. "Say it again, Ana."

"I love you too damn much, Steven."

"Again." He opened his eyes.

"I love you."

Steven nodded to himself, slowly. "Tell me, Anastasia. Am I a good man? Do you trust me to do the right thing? To make the right decision?"

Ana paused. Steven could see the white of her teeth framed between her red lips, could watch the shine of his living room lamp make patterns of light against her jet-black hair. "Yes, Steven," she finally answered. "You're a good man. And I do trust you."

Steven nodded again, this time more vigorously. He took a moment, thought about what he wanted to say. "That's why, Anastasia. . . That's why I have to say goodbye." He allowed himself one brief, dramatic pause. And then, "That's why I'm going on the mission for General Anchorage. Because there are people out there who need my help. And I can't let them down." And he explained the situation to her, as he had a dozen times before: how Steven was the only man who could get the plans to the Allied Command, and how he knew the Tunisian desert like the back of his hand, and how the Free French forces were relying on the information.

She cried. She bawled her little heart out. He was leaving her. Again. But Steven knew that they would be reunited, that three scenes from now, he would emerge victorious, like a man resurrected from the dead, and she would come running into his arms, her red-dress flapping in an invisible breeze, and they would declare their love for each other all over again. And the crowd would appear, and cheer, and scream out his praises, and then disappear, and it would be just the two of them. She the lover, and he the hero. The cast of characters would

19

change, and the villains would rise and fall, but he would always save the day, and she would always be waiting patiently, until they were joyfully reunited. Again and again, and again.

Steven broke off from his reverie. In front of him, Anastasia was shaking her head, a silent *no* on her lips. Steven listened intently. There was a soft sound coming from somewhere. Was it coming from below him? Could he still hear. . . ?

"GLT, play background music for the scene," he commanded. A soft orchestral filled the room. "Now, Anastasia my love," he turned his attention back to the woman in front of him, "where were we?"

About the Author

James Tager is a writer and researcher living in Brooklyn. You can find him haunting his neighborhood coffee shops, buying books and muttering something about 'finishing the ones I already own' to himself, and staring absent-mindedly into space. His fiction has previously been published in *Two Cities Review* and *Gathering Storm Magazine.* You can follow him on Twitter at @jrttager or on Instagram at @jrttiger.

*****~~~~~*****

Down on the Klondike

by David Cleden

CONGRATULATIONS! Your application for a Prospekta control slot has been successful! Fee payable is $999 plus taxes. Opportunity window closes in 3 minutes. Accept/decline?

Since forever, Jamal had dreamed of going to the Moon. Okay, so this wasn't *going* going, but remote telepresence was still way cool. His gaze drifted to the large-scale lunar terrain map covering most of his bedroom wall. In a few places he'd neatly inked in his own name, imagining himself the first human to explore that lunar feature, giving his name to some ridge or rill or impact crater. Pretty lame, but he'd been younger then.

This was different.

Jamal stared at the on-screen message, not quite believing it. 718,492 pending Prospekta applications—and the Lunar Mining Corporation's algorithm had picked him!

Then he remembered—no way could he pay the prospecting fee. Jamal made five bucks an hour on Saturdays, sweeping leaves and neatening Mr. Chernobsky's garden two doors down.

Sighing, Jamal reached for the sticky-note pasted to the underside of his desk, the one with Mom's credit card details that she didn't know he'd copied. He hated going behind her back, but a once-in-a-lifetime chance to drive one of the little klondike rovers? He couldn't pass that up. He'd find a way to pay Mom back. And just suppose he *did* hit paydirt on his shift, unlikely though it was. LMC paid out twenty-K for a confirmed subsurface ice deposit! Sure, it was a fraction of what LMC got for selling the mineral rights on to the United Assembly of Space Agencies, but enough to cover his costs—and then some. Just knowing he'd played a small part in helping site UASA's Lunar Base close to vital ice deposits? That would be priceless.

His phone began lighting up with messages from friends.

>>Jamal! OMG! Just saw they gave you a slot. Crazy!!! You gotta say yes!

>>Hey Jammi. You lucky tush! I've been trying for three years—how'd you do it?

>>You bonehead, Jamal. You're gonna crash and burn!

Then a DM pinged in via public channels, not tagged to his social network.

FROM: 247alien8. *If you're selling, I'll pay x5 face-value, maybe more. Bona fide offer. I represent clients who'll pay big money to queue-jump. Interested? I can better all other offers. Message me back.*

Jamal smiled as he typed a reply. *Thanks, but no thanks. I'm going to the Moon.*

Going to the Moon.

Oh wow. He checked the time-code for his slot allocation.

In fifty-four minutes.

. . .

There was a ton of stuff to read. Legal stuff, codes of conduct, rules and operating procedures, timeout protocols, and revocation clauses. Jamal had already spent days poring over technical manuals for the klondike rovers. He knew the controls inside out.

Klondikes were tough critters. So long as you didn't hurtle around like a lunatic, they couldn't come to much harm. Solar-powered, they were built with standardized components for reliability and redundancy, which also made them easy to mass-produce. LMC paid the bargain-basement rate of a million-plus-change for each one UASA ferried to the Moon. That didn't stop LMC trying to sucker prospectors into signing up for a full damage liability waiver for an additional $1,499 though. No way he was adding *that* to Mom's bill.

Of course, orbiting satellites with ground-penetrating radar and spectrometers had mapped the most likely areas where water might be found, but only klondikes could do the in-situ, high-resolution mapping. In just a few months, UASA would commit to a site for the first permanently manned lunar base. Access to ice reserves was key: water-ice could be cracked into oxygen and hydrogen for breathing, fuel, and much else, in addition to domestic use for the base inhabitants. Undoubtedly there was water on the Moon in low concentrations, locked up in water-ice deposits layered beneath the regolith or lurking in the perpetual shadows of crater rims. Without boots on the ground, tracks on the ground were the next best thing in sniffing it out. LMC's contract with UASA allowed it to sell verified water-ice claims back to UASA for a handsome profit. *How* LMC had chosen to do it was widely regarded as a marketing masterstroke. Crowd-sourcing the survey process via LMC's purpose-built Prospekta app brought the fledgling colonization program something almost as valuable as the trace water-ice deposits themselves: public buy-in. A generation of teenagers, scientifically minded adults, techno-nerd game-players, or the merely curious—all could now play an active role. Each became invested in the success of the lunar base—vital when so many tax dollars were being spent. Everyone was a winner.

Once UASA landed the first batch of 76 klondikes, LMC auctioned off thirty-minute slots, providing direct control of a klondike and its sampler from anywhere on Earth with a decent enough internet connection.

But, thirty minutes. . . It wasn't much. Jamal needed a plan.

A message pinged in the Prospekta app.

Riotgrl26: *Hey! Saw you're allocated to 189. I'll be driving 141. Near neighbors according to the map. Be seeing you! Play nice!*

Jamal checked the historic track of klondike141 in the app. Whoever had control right now seemed clueless, more or less driving in circles and adding no useful measurements. Idiot. He hoped Riotgrl26—whoever that was—would take things a little more seriously.

Jamal decided he would head for a nearby upland region bounded by low hills towards the edge of the eastern prospecting zone. He reckoned fifteen minutes to relocate klondike189 to this mostly unexplored area, then fifteen minutes of prospecting before handing over to some other lucky applicant. He hoped it was a good plan.

Jamal55: *Cool. You too. Feeling kinda nervous right now.*

Riotgrl26: *You'll be fine. Trick with the 3-sec delay is to relax into it. Don't let it bug you or you'll get twitchy and over-compensate. Think s-l-o-w because that's how the klondike will seem.*

Jamal55: *Thanks! See you on the Moon!*

He checked the console time. Two minutes to handover.

His hands felt sweaty on the keyboard. *Please let my internet connection hold up for the next thirty minutes.*

As the last few seconds ticked away, a browser panel came to life with the klondike's camera feed: stark desert-like features rendered in monochrome. Jagged rock formations rose from the gray regolith like teeth from a giant's mouth. Above, the sky was inky black.

A banner flashed in red at the bottom of the screen: CONTROLS ACTIVE!

He was in.

. . .

Things began to go wrong for Jamal less than twelve minutes into the session.

The terrain was more challenging than he'd expected. Klondike189 had entered a sloping plain littered with suitcase-sized rocks. Avoiding them—always allowing for the three-second communications round-trip—meant slower progress, unless he wanted to risk flipping the klondike. At this lower speed, by the time he reached his target zone there would be little time for prospecting.

But the thrill of controlling the klondike left him buzzing. This rock field (frustrating though it was) and the ever-changing view of lunar terrain—Jamal might be the first human to see it up close.

Okay. Decision time. Risk speeding up or change his goal?

He halted the klondike in the inky shadow of a large outcrop and commanded the sensor arm to deploy. On-screen, the articulated arm descended from overhead, touching its probe against regolith. The view jittered briefly, as pneumatics forced the probe a few centimetres below the surface. A reading came back straight away: *Moisture content < 0.03; +/- 17% uncertainty.*

Null reading.

LMC's color chart began with the lowest detectable reading at 0.9 (gray-flagged) and went all the way up to 8.0 (blue), a confirmed strike—detection of subsurface water-ice.

Jamal sighed and retracted the probe. He drove on, repeating the process every couple of minutes. LMC's map updated in real-time, showing his progress as a little breadcrumb trail of white cells signifying the null readings.

Eighteen minutes gone.

Riotgrl26: *How you doing?*

Jamal55: *No luck so far. You?*

Riotgrl26: *Same. Better just enjoy the view I guess.*

He took a moment to pan the camera through three-sixty. A rocky outcrop further north looked most promising, rising perhaps thirty meters above the plain. Some of its deeper clefts could be in perpetual shadow and might theoretically be harboring pockets of millennia-old ice from ancient cometary impacts. But maneuvering the klondike close enough for a sample would be difficult. Easy for the comms-delay to catch him out and risk crunching the rover into a rockface.

Yet it seemed like his best, perhaps only, hope.

He commanded the klondike to approach cautiously, halting on a flattish drift of regolith a few meters from the outcrop. Seven minutes left on the session timer! How had it flown by so quickly? Time enough for two more samples if he was lucky.

He watched the sensor arm extend and bury itself in the regolith.

Moisture content < 0.91; +/- 17% uncertainty. Yellow-flagged residual detection.

Jamal grinned. Yellow was the lowest possible graded result, and not something UASA would get too excited about. But it was *something*. He rolled the klondike forward. Time for one more sample. At least he wouldn't have been completely unlucky.

Moisture content = 1.77; +/- 5% uncertainty. Amber-flagged residual detection. **LMC Ops Centre notified!**

Yes. Yes!

His heart was pounding. An amber hit wasn't too shabby. Again, not uncommon—and certainly no payout—but something he could boast about to his friends.

The session counter showed thirty-five seconds remaining. Better take a last look around. He wouldn't be coming back any time soon.

PRIORITY MESSAGE: LMC Ops Center to Jamal55. *We are pleased to offer you a 30-minute Priority Extend based on your reported measurements. Standard terms and condition apply. Accept/decline?*

He'd heard of this happening. In rare cases LMC would bump everyone down the queue and extend the current session if the algorithms determined a favorable pattern in the klondike's results. *Go get the job done*, they were saying. Many commentators said it was a sly move. LMC already had you on the hook for a grand and now they dangled more bait in front of you. The payout was twenty big ones for a confirmed blue strike...

Of course, LMC took another session fee regardless of the outcome. They were smart like that.

247alien8: *Hey kid. You wanna sell your new slot? I've got clients willing to pay TEN times face value. All legal and above board.*

Jamal hesitated. Ten thousand dollars was a lot of money, more than he'd "borrowed" from Mom. But this wasn't just about the money, was it?

Jamal55: *Nope.*

With barely a twinge of guilt he reached for Mom's credit card details again and paid the session fee.

. . .

The trick, Jamal thought, was to approach from an oblique angle. If the comms delay tripped him, he'd be less likely to ram the klondike into a rock-face. He needed to get close, but not *that* close. And the damage liability penalty—

Okay, best not to think about *that*.

He drove the klondike up a gently rising slope of regolith, until the gray-black rock-face began to fill the screen. Stopping, he panned the camera downwards to check the sample site. He noticed a darker patch of regolith in a slight depression a meter further on. Probably nothing, but darker coloration could be an indicator of subsurface ice-layers.

He commanded the klondike forward one meter, watching the camera's view wobble into motion three seconds later. Now to deploy the sensor arm—

The camera image jerked wildly. The rock-face tilted at a jaunty angle—and kept on tilting. Jamal sent a frantic autostop command even though the klondike wasn't in powered drive.

The camera view grew confused. For an instant he glimpsed the blue-white disk of Earth hanging above a sharply defined horizon, then it was lost in a dust swirl. The image began glitching with dropouts.

Holy crap. The klondike was *falling*. The sliver of horizon was receding, darkness closing in on all sides, and now the picture was fritzing all to hell with signal-loss, then—

Nothing.

WARNING! Your connection to Klondike189 has unexpectedly terminated. Please contact a LMC customer advisor to determine cause and liability for loss. Without legal liability indemnity, be advised that klondike replacement value is currently set at $1.4 million.

Jamal put his head in his heads.

. . .

247alien8: *Hey buddy. Need some help?*

Jamal ignored the message. He needed to *think*. Cave systems were known to exist on the Moon. Many were formed by ancient lava tubes; caverns left behind after basaltic lava drained away millions of years ago. The klondike must have broken through a thin surface crust and tumbled down.

If so, there was no way to recover his klondike. No way to even make contact with surface relay towers from below ground. And the replacement cost... Several lifetimes' worth of lawn-sweeping for Mr. Chernobsky.

Riotgrl26: *Hey. What happened?*

Jamal55: *Think I just fell down a deep, dark rabbit-hole.*

He was feeling sick to the bottom of his stomach. If he hadn't nudged the klondike forward for that final reading. . .

Riotgrl26: *Those pesky moon-rabbits. Hold on. Let me see if I can get close enough to piggy-back the visuals from your klondike.*

Minutes dragged while Jamal stared at the grayed out camera feed. Then the picture jumped, fritzing with jittery lines. Stabilized.

Riotgrl26: *That's as close as I dare get.*

Jamal55: *I have a connection again!*

In its headlight beam, the camera showed the klondike on its side. A miracle it was still in one piece, really. Perhaps he could use the sensor arm to push the klondike upright again? He panned the camera, getting his bearings.

Just meters away, the cavern broadened and deepened. He'd been lucky. If the klondike had tumbled any further it would almost certainly be out of Riotgrl26's signal reach. Not that it made any difference. Short of levitation, there was no way to get the klondike out of there. The rover was lost—and Jamal was squarely on the hook.

But catching the headlight beam, the cave walls sparkled, like some vast, jewel-encrusted art-installation. Everywhere he looked—a cave of wonders.

Ice crystals.

Riotgrl26: *I'm seeing it! This is awesome!*

Jamal couldn't believe it. The stuff dreams were made of—if only the circumstances were more favorable.

Jamal's phone vibrated. *Unknown caller.* Surely not LMC chasing for the klondike replacement fee already? He snatched it up.

"Hello?"

"You know me as 247alien8, kid. I'm a lawyer specialising in off-earth mineral exploitation contracts, and I'm about to save your skinny ass."

Jamal sighed. A lawyer. Who said things couldn't get any worse?

"Don't—I repeat—don't take a sensor reading yet. First establish incontrovertibly with LMC you are below ground. Get video capture of the lava tube, the surface break, the cavern, everything. You don't want your klondike logging a surface location."

"I don't?"

"My advice is about to make you a millionaire. Do you trust me?"

"I guess."

"Good. I'll take that as your consent to me acting as your legal representative. My fee will be five percent of whatever stake-money you get. Agreed?"

"I guess."

"Kid, LMC don't hold subsurface claim rights. It's a contract loophole UASA inserted. LMC are licensed for surface claims only—sold back to UASA for a handsome price—which, by the way, is way more than the stake-money paid to the discoverer. But *you* can sell a sub-surface claim to UASA directly. Cut LMC out and they don't have to pocket their enormous fee. Sound good?"

"I guess."

"Can you say anything else?"

"I can't believe it's that simple."

"It's economics. Successful prospectors get their cut, but LMC takes a bigger one. So does UASA ultimately. The lunar base will be a stepping stone to commercial asteroid capture and mineral extraction worth literally *billions* in the final analysis. It's market forces all the way down the chain. And I'll help you leverage your share."

"The klondike—"

"We'll offer LMC market value out of the claim fee. Maybe one percent over, just to keep things smooth."

Jamal hesitated. "What about Riotgrl26? She's the only reason I've still got contact."

"Your call, kid. Cut her in if that's what you want."

"I do."

"Okay. So make sure you've logged your camera-feed, take the damn readings and make us all rich."

. . .

It wasn't that simple, though. First Jamal had to right the klondike using its sensor arm. He worried that the sensor package might have been damaged in the fall. And what if their assumptions were wrong, if this was something other than water-ice? He could still be in debt to LMC to the tune of $1.4 million.

But the reading came back not just blue, it was the highest tagged, double-A++ blue-rating possible. Such high concentrations were unprecedented. He imagined a klaxon going off in the LMC Ops Center.

"As my lawyer," Jamal said, "I want you to do something for me." He rushed on before he could change his mind. "Use whatever you need from the stake money—all of it if necessary—but I'd like the cavern complex officially named after me as the discoverer." He felt his face flush with embarrassment.

247alien8 laughed. "Sure. Why not? If that's what you want."

It was. It seemed likely this would be a prime candidate for siting the lunar base. Generations of colonists might get to know this place, but he would always be the first to have seen it.

And the next version of the lunar map on his wall would look mighty fine with his name on it.

"There's one thing that's not negotiable, kid."

Jamal felt his heart sink.

"I'm going to advance you—right now—a percentage of what's due to you when UASA pays out. It won't seem like much—but enough to treat your Mom to something special. I mean *really* special. Because, boy do you have a lot of explaining to do, kid."

###

About the Author

David Cleden is a British SF/F writer, and this marks his fourth appearance in a Third Flatiron anthology. His work has also appeared in venues such as Interzone, Galaxy's Edge, Analog, Deep Magic, Cossmass Infinities, Metaphorosis, and Writers of the Future Volume 35. He was the winner of the 2016 James White Award and the Aeon Award (2017). He has previously worked in satellite remote sensing and earth observation, which left him convinced his to-be-read book pile must now be visible from low earth orbit. He has a website at www.quantum-scribe.com and can be found on Twitter as @davidcleden.

*****~~~~~*****

Sunrunner

by Robert Bagnall

As her solar-jeep slowed to a crawl, Parra realized she'd just swapped one problem for another. In escaping Amparor's bounty hunters, she had crossed into the penumbra. Forced into arbitrary choices, she had swung off the blacktop and along a track, grit giving way to two grey stripes an axel's width apart, stripes which gradually greened, then yellowed as the route ascended and the trees thinned, and the ground turned bare and sandy, the track barely visible, until here she was.

Which was where, exactly?

She looked about her. Above the tree line, she approached a saddle between rolling scrub-grass hills, the ground rising further to her right and falling away to the left into a vast valley of olives and pine. Behind her, the dust she'd kicked up settled. Above her, high in the atmosphere, hung floating suncatchers, Amparor's solar-powered airships with mirrored sails, like insects with monstrous wings but minuscule bodies. They formed a swarm, many miles across, casting the territory around her into midday twilight as they deflected the sunlight to power generators and intensive farms. And, as the sun sank, the shadow would extend ever further over her.

She watched and waited, peering into the gloaming for signs of being followed. Satisfied, she chugged water, slid the bottle back into the jeep between sleeping roll and kitbag, acutely aware she was down to three bottles. Then she slipped off her shorts and, in the lee of the jeep, urinated, the tension of the chase, the escape, leeching from her.

The obvious solution was to lock the jeep's comsdish onto the nearest suncatcher, hack the protocols, realign a mirror or two and beam a pool of sunlight onto the vehicle's solar array, to recharge the batteries. But that was madness. Even if Amparor's men failed to spot the errant beam of sunlight picking out Parra's position like a rock star's solo, the hack would swiftly yield up her exact coordinates. Better to trickle-charge in the half-light and see how far she could get at the pace of a funeral cortege.

An hour later, with the batteries out of the red, she nursed the jeep towards the brow of the hill. The track had petered out, and she was now picking the smoothest path between boulders. She paused before the ridge, scanned the miles of ground behind her, then climbed the last fifty yards to recce what was to come.

The other side of the ridge was a sea of weak and weedy bracken and ferns. Down below, in a secluded cleft, an ancient Winnebago formed the core of a Rube Goldberg habitation, as if in the process of decaying, structures had sprouted forth organically, like overnight fungi. A small wind turbine turned lazily. Chickens clucked around the ghost of a station wagon, down on its axels, a wooden ramp built up to its open rear. A stream ran nearby, and around it the ground had been tilled and terraced, forming a small field planted out with waist-high maize and jaundiced greens.

As Parra watched, a willowy girl emerged from the Winnebago and, carrying bowls, strode over to the chickens. In an adjoining pen, two pigs, blotched black, waddled into view, expectant. The girl scattered grains to the poultry and kitchen scraps to the porkers. With the livestock occupied, she busied herself mucking out, a wisp of a whistled tune wafting up the hillside. And then, prompted by nothing at all, she looked straight up at where Parra stood on the hillside. And froze.

A quarter of a mile away, Parra felt their eyes lock. She guessed at the girl's emotions: anger at being watched, confusion at what the intrusion meant, fear of what comes next. Parra raised a hand, open palmed, showing she meant no threat, but all it did was send the girl running back inside, her rake dropped amongst the clucking hens.

In the jeep, Parra coasted downhill, pushing through the bracken outcrops. As she pulled up an unthreatening distance from the RV, the reception committee emerged. All two of them. A woman, bird-like and scrawny, an unkempt mass of curly hair, dressed in a grubby shift with a shotgun under her arm, and behind her, the chicken-feeding girl. The woman walked with a wobble. Parra guessed at sixty for her age and then, for reasons she couldn't quite define, revised it downwards to forty-something. Forty-something and ill. Even armed, she looked like Parra could simply stroll over and push her to the ground.

"I just need to recharge. I don't need any food. Just water. I'll be gone tomorrow. . . "

"If you're flat, you'll need a full day, at least," the woman cut in, glancing first at the jeep, then skywards, glowering at the perpetual gloom. For all her hobo looks, it was a confident, refined voice. The muzzle of the shotgun drooped.

"Day after, tops, then," Parra assured. Hidden in this valley, another day may put distance between her and Amparor's bounty hunters. Or give them time to find her.

The woman chewed her cheeks, considering the matter, and asked Parra whether she had any coffee. When Parra said she did, she was told to bring it to the Winnebago.

From the state of the Winnebago's exterior, Parra feared what she might find: a hand-to-mouth subsistence existence, a reclaimed trash aesthetic, dog shit in the rugs. She paused at the entrance, and not just because June, the willowy girl, asked her to remove her shoes. To her right, the kitchen was spartan, but spotless. The lower half of an espresso maker sat on an induction ring, the water heating, awaiting the addition of Parra's ground arabica. To her left: Berber caravan meets fin de siècle Paris, a boudoir of batik throws and paisley ottomans, of sandalwood and incense smoke. The sick woman—Claudia—was now wearing a once-elegant garment in red and gold velvet. The soles of her feet were dirty, and Parra wondered what lengths she would go to cleaning up afterwards—or was it hidden by the proliferation of pattern? The shotgun sat propped in a corner, incongruous.

"Haven't had coffee for a while," Claudia said, taking the pack and spooning grounds into the espresso-maker. She screwed it back together whilst on the ring, her fingertips gingerly holding the hot lower section. "We used to both go down the valley. Trade. Buy supplies. Carry them back together. But I'm not so good right now." She caught her breath and grimaced at the labor of coffee making.

June sat half on, half off a large patchwork footstool, like she was the visitor, concerned but not surprised. She was idly playing with the shotgun. At Parra's concerned look, she admitted they hadn't had any shells for months.

"What is it you got?" Parra asked Claudia.

Claudia shrugged. "I'm not wasting dollars on a doctor to tell me what I can guess."

"I can drive you somewhere. When I'm charged."

With an effort, Claudia busied herself searching the cupboard. Matching mugs mattered, it seemed. June brightened. "She can drive us down the valley. And back."

Three complementing cups found, Claudia shook her head and said she would die there, then added for June's benefit, "She meant drive us someplace different, to live a different life for you. For me, to die in comfort."

"I meant to buy supplies," Parra said. "Medicine."

"Too late for medicine," Claudia said wistfully. The pungent smell of fresh coffee filled the galley. "Hope you like it black. We don't have any milk. Would have liked a cow." She was already regretting what wasn't yet over.

"The suncatchers here when you arrived?" Parra asked.

The woman shook her head, her expression suggesting history. "They were on the horizon, but they spread. We never see the sun no more, not fully."

Cups in hand, they moved to the Winnebago's lounge-end, where June declared as if a fundamental truth had been revealed to her, "You're a sunrunner, aren't you?"

Sunrunner. Parra had been called worse. Like 'terrorist'. She nodded. No point denying it. She guessed the girl had seen the military-grade comsdish, that Parra was on the run, put two and two together.

Claudia snorted. "No such thing, a modern-day myth."

Indignant, June said she'd seen the beams of stolen sunlight in the gloom. "I saw them last night. I was at the top of the ridge. It was like angels from heaven."

Their eyes sought out Parra, whose silence couldn't help but confirm her part in it.

"So you steal the sun back from Amparor Incorporated and give it to the poor, like some solar Robin Hood?" Claudia said. "What's in it for you?"

"Sunlight should be free," Parra said. "Like the air."

"I've read about it, Mamma," June brightened. "There are even people in the cities who don't want

37

twenty-four-hour sunlight, who know it's stolen, who want the natural rhythms of the world, who want us to have our sunlight back. . . "

"Sure, there are philanthropists who would like to see us succeed, who help us," Parra confirmed.

Claudia was skeptical. "But don't you just work for some other Amparor? Some other power company? Doesn't it all go to a power plant or industrial farm in the end?"

Parra shrugged. "I've freelanced for the corporates. There's some of my code on those winged beasts up there. Girl's gotta eat. But not always. Sometimes I hack the suncatchers because—"

"—because it's the right thing to do?" Claudia laughed disbelievingly.

Parra shook her head. "Because I like beating people like Amparor Incorporated."

. . .

Parra had three steaks in an icebox in the jeep that she feared might already have powered down. She was happy to share; these two both looked like they had gone too long without decent nutrition, even if in Claudia's case it would just be holding back the inevitable. The smallholding had vegetables and, of course, the chickens. "Steak and eggs and a side salad," declared Claudia. "Can't call it a green salad. More of a sallow salad."

Over dinner June interrogated Parra over the suncatchers, as if Parra worked for Amparor Incorporated, and not against them: how she hacked the suncatcher's code, how she repositioned their mirrors to provide light and heat and power to the disenfranchised, how they stayed up in the air. She was explaining how they electrolyzed water vapor in the atmosphere into hydrogen and oxygen, then used the lighter-than-air hydrogen to maintain buoyancy, when June blurted, "You got a price on your head? Alive or dead?"

Parra wondered whether her directness was nature or nurture, how much contact she'd really had with the outside world. She caught Claudia's beady eye studying her. She was curious, too. "It's true they'd rather I didn't do what I do," she said.

"Mamma says she misses the limelight more than the sunlight."

The change in subject was abrupt but not unwelcome. "Actress?"

"Dancer," Claudia said. "Ballet."

It made sense. Her lithe movements, her bohemian sangfroid.

Claudia waved it away. "It was all a long time ago."

"Mamma danced Swan Lake with the New York City Ballet. . . "

". . . in the company."

"But you were the swan."

Parra enjoyed the exchange between mother and daughter, like it was a performance itself, Claudia torn between modesty and the need to clarify. "*A* swan. Not *the* swan. I was never the prima ballerina. I rehearsed the dying swan, but never performed it."

"But you were good enough."

"Darling, we were *all* good enough."

. . .

The next day, as the milky light recharged the jeep's batteries, Parra sat in a borrowed deckchair and pored over code. There is a naïve belief hacking is like picking a lock, a password stumbled upon like the twist of a hairpin and open sesame. But Parra had to have her patches and worms prepared in advance, ready to insert into operating instructions. Her kludges were designed to do two things: delay Amparor from regaining control of the mirrors; and minimize the digital breadcrumbs that could lead back to her. The irony that sunlight theft was, quite literally, spotlighted was never lost on her.

All the time she worked, as the chickens clucked and the pigs snuffled and the stream burbled and the smell of earth and animals hung in the breeze, a thought nagged away at her. Initially, she wasn't even aware of it, mistaking it for irritation at the continuous slow hollow knock-knock-knock of a wind chime. But then she realized it wasn't that—it was what Claudia had said the evening before.

Her fingers froze over the keyboard. She hated it when a part of her mind detached, floated free with its own agenda. Easier to meet it halfway, find a solution, refocus.

No, it wasn't what she had said. It was *how* she said it, the note of wistful regret. It was what she *hadn't said.* She was never the prima ballerina—and now, *never would be.*

Parra shook her head to clear the pressure of the idea that was forming. All the shrewd, logical, rational, prudent, judicious, risk-calculating parts of her screamed it was stupid, stupid, stupid. But she knew whichever part of her id held the casting vote would ensure she would do exactly that.

Because it was *the right thing to do.*

. . .

It took Parra four hours to code, dimly aware of June bustling between crops and livestock. She had to pick when the routine would execute, not just dusk, but the exact time, to the second, and work backwards. She would have no chance to test, to finesse, to correct. But that was fine. The greatest risk was if it worked.

She made it with twenty minutes to spare, the buzz in her head telling her she'd been running on empty. The dimness that had descended all around her came as a shock. She could get like that coding: head down, batting back problems of logic and sequence to the detriment of real-world distractions like food and water.

She opened the Winnebago's door, rapped on the aluminum architrave. Claudia lay on the couch, glassy-eyed, neither asleep nor awake. June sat in the gloom nearby, equally inert. They were like machinery on standby. Parra wondered about the sense of what she was about to do.

"Could you. . . join me out here?" she asked, nodding to the darkness behind.

Still bare-footed, Claudia took the steps slowly, one-at-a-time, stooped, but trying not to let her tiredness show. "Are you off? Are you not going to wait until morning?" Behind her, June had the shotgun crooked under her arm like she was off coney-hunting.

In the lower atmosphere some miles away, a mirrored array on a suncatcher's wing flipped, deflecting the evening sunlight travelling almost parallel to the surface of the earth below. Magic hour light, like liquid gold, it beamed towards a second floating, flying airship-butterfly that passed it to a third, overhead, its mirrors also under Parra's control.

A heartbeat later, the beam of warm light, three feet wide, descended from the darkness above, perfectly placed between Winnebago and animal enclosures.

Claudia stiffened. In the dimness Parra couldn't tell what she was thinking.

From the solar-jeep's stereo, the sound of Saint-Saens' *Le Cygne* filled the air. Parra fell back further into the gloom. This was not her moment.

The aged dancer looked briefly to her daughter, as if for permission. Even in the half-light, Parra sensed June's eyes wordlessly say, *Go on, Mamma.*

Claudia stepped into the light, barefoot, en pointe, stretched, and transformed from woman to swan. As the music glided, she fluttered and flickered, surged and swayed, her legs giving the most delicate of kicks as her arms arced like wings. She never once left the light, but gave the impression of flying, rising, high into the sky.

41

And, as the music reached its quiet crescendo, she folded into the dirt, her arms over her head, and lay still.

"Mighty impressive," said a whiskey-soaked, tobacco-stained voice.

In the shadows June spun, the shotgun ready for action. Claudia lay inert. Parra froze. The man stepped forward, his own snub-nosed weapon brandished. Bounty hunter.

"I've orders to take you in," he said to June. Parra realized he thought June was the sunrunner. The spotlight beam, still shining down on the prostrate Claudia, had dazzled him. He hadn't seen Parra in the darkness, and June's shotgun was now taking all the attention. And if she remained still, he probably still wouldn't see her. But when the time-limited routine that held the suncatchers captive expired in a matter of a minute or so and the beam blinked out of existence—what would happen then?

He'd fire, that's what, Parra reasoned.

"Mamma," June cried and fell to her knees by her mother.

"What the—?" the bounty hunter declared, now uncertain who this was in front of him.

"She's dead. Mamma's dead."

Parra knew this was the moment she had to emerge, make sure the bounty-hunter knew Claudia and June were not his targets, even if that meant giving herself up.

Unless. . .

She slunk behind her jeep, revived the laptop, and dimmed the screen. She had thirty seconds, tops. In theory, all she had to do was add a string of zeros to a key parameter or two, nudge the settings a fraction of an arcsecond, reconfigure, re-run the routine, pray the first suncatcher in the chain, high in the sky and way to the west, was still bathed in the last of the evening light. That and. . .

42

"Hey," she shouted, springing up from behind the jeep. She didn't want the man to have his weapon pointed at June, now draped crying over her mother's body.

CRACK! As the spotlight beam disappeared, the man fired. Parra was ready for it, ducking, the shot going wide.

In the darkness, she reemerged from behind the jeep, arms high. "It's me you want. The girl's nothing to do with this." She stepped forward. She needed him to do the same.

She counted down in her head. *Ten, nine. . .*

She needed him to step forward—assuming the sun had not yet sunk.

"You don't have orders to take me in. You've orders to take me down. So do it."

Rile him, Parra thought. The man inched forward. Not enough.

Five, four, three. . .

Parra sprung and rolled and dived into the darkness.

The man stepped forward and fired at where she had been.

As he did so, another beam shot down from the suncatcher above. But this was no prima ballerina's stage illumination. This was pencil thin, the sun's ferocity distilled. It struck the bounty hunter square in the top of his head and followed his spine earthwards. He was dead before he collapsed, with all the finality but none of Claudia's grace.

A moment later the beam was gone, a mirror shattered somewhere high above, Parra guessed. There was a seared barbeque tang on the air. She followed the sound of sobbing, and as her eyes became accustomed to the gloom, put her arms around June who declared, "She died dancing. She died happy. She died in the limelight."

###

About the Author

Robert Bagnall was born in a doubly-landlocked English county when the Royal Navy still issued a rum ration, but now lives by the sea. He is the author of the science fiction thriller, *2084—The Meschera Bandwidth*, and around fifty published short stories, twenty-four of which are collected in the anthology, *24 0s & a 2*. Both are available on Amazon. Three of his stories have also appeared in NewCon Press's annual "Best of British Science Fiction" anthologies. He blogs at meschera.blogspot.com and can be contacted there.

*****~~~~~*****

Moving On

by Andrew Wright

Harry Walsh sat on the chair of his porch, sipping his coffee, waiting for the moment when inspiration would strike. That golden moment when he would be ready to start the day. Sometimes it came quickly, sometimes not. Today felt like it might take a while. In the meantime he would stare at the ocean and enjoy the view.

Time was. He hadn't been married long then. Time was when he couldn't even see the sea from his front porch, hidden as it was by the pine trees. Now it was just a few minutes walk to go for a swim. Every cloud has a silver lining.

He looked to his left as tire noise heralded an approaching U-Haul van pulling a large trailer. It slowed and then halted in front of a house. The driver's window rolled down and Ben Smith leaned out.

"Hey there, Harry," he said.

"Hey yourself, Ben," said Harry, "I heard talk that you were shipping out."

"Well, you heard right," said Ben.

"Where you heading for?" Harry walked over to the van.

"Thought we'd try our luck in Juneau."

"That figures. You got friends or family up there?"

"Nah. But the relocation program is pretty good. Not as generous as it used to be but enough to get a roof over our heads."

"What you planning on doing up there?"

"Got a job fruit-picking. Should be ok 'til I get something better."

Harry had heard that plenty often before—most people who said it were still picking fruit in the Alaskan countryside.

"Well, I hope it works out for you, Ben," said Harry, thinking that maybe it wouldn't.

"When you planning on getting outta here, Harry?"

"No time soon," he replied.

"The Cape's finished, Harry," said Ben.

"Maybe, but I don't think I've got it in me to start over."

"Well, we've got a boat to catch so I'll wish you all the best—don't wanna be stuck here for the storm!"

"Ok, Ben, take care now."

The Cape finished? Harry snorted. Cape Cod was finished years ago. The cod disappeared in the twenties, and it stopped being a cape ten years later when Highways gave up the battle to keep the causeway open. Apparently nobody saw the irony in the new name—Cape Cod Island.

He went back and finished his coffee then he sentenced himself to do the rounds of the houses—his least favorite job. But he needed to do it before the storm arrived.

Back in the day, a tiny beachfront cottage would sell for north of a million and a large family home would be five or even ten. Boston's wealthy would slip quietly in for a summer of rest, seafood and local wines. Wines not beefed up on grapes from California, seeing that Massachusetts could grow all the fruit it needed. That was when Harry and his wife made a good living.

Those houses and their owners were long gone now. The houses claimed by the sea as it marched inland, little by little each year—taking first a dock and then a boathouse or a storage shed. The ignorant battled at first, shoring up the ends of their gardens with attractive arrangements of wooden logs and trees planted so their roots would hold the soil in place and then, when this failed, with steel sheet piles driven in for mile after clanging mile. The wisest sold up more or less straight away, accepting their losses there and then. Of course, the sea eventually took the houses on the front line leaving the less desirable houses behind; the smaller dwellings promoted from the role of best supporting actor to lead, by virtue of the winter storms. Rank upon rank succumbed and prices tumbled faster than the gable ends.

Now one of Harry's many jobs was to tour some twenty properties on a weekly basis and report on any damage done by the encroaching sea. Truth was that in the spring and summer he usually only went round every few weeks unless there was a storm and then, oh boy, whole houses could disappear overnight. And there was a storm on the way today. Not a big one but bad enough.

Harry's main job was to predict if something was going to become unsafe and advise on whether that something should be fixed or abandoned. When he checked, he always walked right past the house and into the garden to see if any more of it had dropped into the sea since he'd last been there. When a storm was approaching he took the precaution of driving colored wooden pegs into the soil at six feet intervals—red, white and blue. That way, when he went back, he could quickly assess the damage. He always took a 'before' picture. None of it made any difference to the outcome of course, but his customers felt he was in command of the situation

47

and continued to pay him the small fee that he charged. That was the important thing when you were scraping a living any way you could.

It took a couple of hours to go round all of the houses, drive the pegs in, and have a quick look round each building to see if there was any obvious damage. It was dull work—all the more so for being completely futile. The sea would win in the end. It always did. Since he'd begun offering this service to the good people of Cape Cod, he'd watched a hundred and three properties fall into the sea. As a business, it had a limited life span.

He was debating whether to go on to another house or stop at his favorite (and the only) diner for a quick coffee when his cell phone rang and saved him making a decision.

"Harry?" It was Courtney, his wife.

"Hi, darling, how's it going?"

"I'm fine, sweetie, but Sadie has a problem." Sadie O'Donnell was his wife's best friend. "She's got the builders in, repairing a hole in her roof. They've lashed a tarpaulin over their work, but one of the ropes has worked loose and it's flapping about like a codfish on a boat deck."

"I'll go right over," said Harry.

"Oh, would you? You are a darling, Harry."

"I guess I am a bit special," he joked.

"I heard the Smiths were leaving for Alaska."

"Yes, so I hear." That killed the mood.

"I'm just saying," she said.

"I don't have time for an argument." It was old ground and well trodden. She wanted to talk about leaving, and he didn't. A sore point picked over so often that it was too painful to touch.

It wasn't five minutes drive to Sadie's. As he opened the car door he could hear the tarpaulin whipping back and forth making a sound like a gigantic flag flapping in a breeze. He didn't knock on the door, just grabbed a ladder from the back of his pick up and went round the back of the house to where the noise was coming from.

It took him a few attempts to catch the flailing rope, but he finally grabbed it and lashed it to one of the fence posts where the railing round the deck came close to the house. He gave a good pull on the rope to make sure it was solid and took the ladder back to the pick-up. He was heading back home to get some lunch and wasn't even planning to knock on Sadie's door, but she opened it and hollered for him to come and get a coffee.

Harry turned and headed for the house. He liked Sadie's company. She led him into the kitchen to pour him a coffee. Like many of the houses on the Cape, it was decorated with sailing and fishing paraphernalia—mainly pictures of someone holding the one that didn't get away.

Back in the day Sophie used to run a thirty-eight footer, charter fishing out of Provincetown. She and her husband, Mike, would take groups fishing for bass and cod or sometimes just whale watching, for those of a less predatory bent. As fish stocks changed they'd changed too, first looking for dorado and even sailfish until these too headed north and they moved on to tarpon and barracuda. Mike used to joke that the only thing that hadn't come from the Caribbean was the reggae.

Mike had struggled to cope with the setbacks and hardships. He'd turned to drink and things had fallen apart. Courtney had spent many long evenings helping Sadie cope with Mike's drinking and then helping her cope with the divorce.

Sadie handed Harry his drink.

"You all set for the storm?" she said.

"Guess so," he said.

"Got your boat out?"

Harry didn't have the temperament for taking tourists out on boats, but he still made a living on the water. While Sadie and Mike had been schmoozing

Boston bankers, Harry was chasing a dwindling supply of lobsters or scallops. He always seemed to have the knack for joining an activity just as it fizzled out. After the lobsters disappeared he moved on to stone crabs but numbers didn't rise fast enough to meet the demands of the large number of fishermen fighting off poverty and the crab population crashed before it had even got started.

So, like some bad joke, he'd invested heavily in shrimping gear during the exact same year that sales of wild-caught shrimp were banned because of micro-plastic. He might as well have taken his savings out in cash and thrown them onto the fire. Not that he blamed them for the ban. He blamed micro-plastic for Courtney's cancer. Sadie had been an absolute rock when they went through that.

He managed to hold onto the boat even after the house was repossessed and they'd moved into the smaller place that they still had now. Now he used the boat to ferry people and supplies around.

"Boat's down by Bass River, she'll be fine down there," said Harry.

"Didn't you hear the forecast? Winds backing to the east."

"Northeast," corrected Harry.

"No, it shifted. They definitely said it's going to blow in from the east."

There was a sinking feeling in Harry's stomach. The safe place he'd berthed his boat would not be so well protected from an easterly wind.

"Shit, guess I missed that update," he said, putting his coffee cup down, "I'll have to move fast to get the boat out before the weather starts in."

"Need a hand?" she asked.

"Nope, so long as I look smart, I'll be ok," he said, heading out of the door.

Bass River used to be a broad inlet with shallow edges surrounded by broadleaved trees. Perfect for a lazy day of not catching fish whilst drinking beers and shooting the breeze. Back then a boat moored there would be protected whatever direction the wind blew from but now it was a different story.

The trees were long gone. Oak, beech and ash had disappeared like the wealthy tourists as the climate went from warm to hot to baking in the summer. So, the lack of trees and the rising water level meant that boats could no longer snuggle down beneath the shelter of the woods on the riverbank. If the wind blew from the north or northeast it wasn't too bad as waves washed over land too far away to affect the boats. But if it came from the east or the south east then a heavy swell would roll along the river, and it was a brave owner who would leave a boat moored there. He needed to get his boat out of the water—pronto!

He raced back home as fast as the potholed roads would allow. He was hooking up the trailer as Courtney came out of the house.

"What're you doing?" she asked.

"I've got to get the boat out. Wind's shifting to the east and I've left it by the bridge at Bass River."

"I'm coming with you," she said.

"No. There's no need."

It would be helpful to have her along, but it would also be an admission of how difficult things were. He didn't need to give his wife that kind of ammunition.

"Harry, I'm not having you trying to winch the boat out in a swell all on your own. Please."

She knew him too well. Please don't be defensive. Please don't choose something as serious as this as a battleground. Please let me care for you.

"Come on then, but hurry," he said, helpless against the word.

It was less than a mile away and, as they climbed out of the car, the wind made their coats flap and Courtney's hair dance wildly around her face.

They could see the swell rolling along the river, not ready to do much damage yet but with growing menace. Some of the waves out in the middle of the river had white tips, and little bits of sea foam were being blown across the water. Getting out to the boat would be a dangerous prospect.

So, it was good job that Harry didn't have to do that. He stood at the edge of the water and took out his phone. He used the Pilot app to start the engine. Swinging the boat round to face the incoming swell, he began to reel in the anchor as Courtney reversed the trailer to the water's edge. Soon the anchor was free and Harry began to inch the boat over to where Courtney was slowly pushing the trailer under the water ready to for the boat.

Harry grabbed the winch cable and unwound a good length. He would need to wade into the water a bit to attach the cable to the boat but that was a damn sight less dangerous than having to take a tender or swim out to it. His waders would keep his feet dry.

He brought the boat nearer. At the last moment he would have to swing it round to bring it onto the trailer bow first. That would be the tricky part, because doing this would bring the boat side on to the swell and the boat would rock quite a bit. Still, if he judged it right and did it quickly, it would be ok. Maybe he'd have to steady the boat with his hands a little, but once he got the cable attached and Courtney started to winch it in, the boat would soon come under control. He positioned himself so that he would be at the other side of the boat from the direction that the swell came from. That way he could push back as the swell tried to turn the boat.

He looked back to the truck. Courtney was looking through the rear windscreen, concentrating hard. He smiled and waved to reassure her. It wasn't risky—worse thing that could happen was being shoved out of the way by the boat and having to start again.

The boat was close enough now. Time to swing it round. He was looking at the swell beyond the boat. Judging the moment.

Now! He swung the boat round and powered it towards him. Then, as he readied the clip to attach the cable, he felt something rub the top of his rubber boot. He looked down absent-mindedly. In the trough of the waves he could just about make out his foot.

He saw his foot had slipped under a—what was it? He laughed, because he recognized the piece of metal. It was part of a radiator. Not just any radiator, this was part of a specially crafted radiator that had once warmed Sally Maskell's house. Sally Maskell was a multi-millionaire and had commissioned special, 'artsy' chrome radiators for her living room to keep her warm if she came out during the autumn. She loved the design, but Harry and the plumber thought they were truly awful. That was some ten years ago, and then, just five years after that, the whole house had slid into Bass River over a period of just five weeks after a string of storms moved up the East Coast. Harry half smiled as he recognized it and pulled his foot out of the way.

Except his foot didn't move.

Concerned now he pulled again. His foot was wedged under the metal pipe and he began to worry that he might put a hole in the rubber boot and ruin an expensive pair of waders. Then he looked up.

A larger wave had hit the boat broadside and pushed it over towards Harry. Normally it wouldn't take a great effort to push the boat away, and himself from it, but the boat had been lifted by the swell and was coming back down fast—at him.

Harry tried to push back, but 6,000 lbs of moving boat was very unforgiving. It pushed him over and under the water, rubbing him between the hull and the river bottom like a seed in a grinder. And the floor of Sally Maskell's demolished house was anything but smooth. In a few painful seconds Harry's life was snuffed out.

Courtney saw the whole thing happen through the rain spattered truck window. She barely had time to raise her hand to her mouth before it was over, the froth on the waves turning from white to pink and Harry floating slowly away, face down in the water, missing one of his rubber boots (still containing his foot, as it later turned out).

Courtney felt but didn't really recognize the feelings of anger and jealousy that flitted through her just before blind panic set in. That first flash of emotion was the recognition that Harry had managed to escape the Cape before her. In an instant she recognized that now she would never escape. Not until the last inch of the island was swallowed by the ocean.

About the Author

Andrew Wright is a part-time science teacher living in York, England, with a wife and two dogs, waiting for the world to calm down again so that we can do some more travelling.

*****~~~~~*****

To Vanquish Other Blooms

by Tim Borella

Something metallic pings off the windscreen, making me flinch. A glinting speck ricochets away, leaving a star in the glass.

"Damn bee," says Jonas, the farmhand driving me out to the site. "They're supposed to be able to dodge things, but they ain't that great at it sometimes."

Masses of them swirl around the sunflowers like sparks over a fire. Ten thousand assigned to this crop alone, according to the deployment records. It'd eat up any profit if this wasn't a government thing. Better than the alternative, though.

"I'll take you round the perimeter track to where your boss is set up," Jonas says. "How long you here for, anyway?"

"A week or so. Depends on what we find."

"And what is it you're looking for?"

"Nothing special. Just a progress survey. You know how managers love stats."

"Ain't that the truth."

He hasn't mentioned the workplace incident, as we're calling it. That's good. Better if people don't speculate too much before we know what's going on ourselves. There's that need-to-know principle we invoke so often.

The thought makes me grimace. I thought the secrecy was cool early on, classified files and whatnot, but the longer I spend in this job the more I see how screwed up things really are. It's not the public we protect with our spin, it's ourselves, or more accurately, the upper echelons.

Working for Karen Coppick doesn't help. I was a fan of her early research and pushed hard to get on her team, but the reality didn't live up to the hype. She talks the talk, but it's hollow. She may have been passionate once, but clearly she's done with being a real worker and is aiming higher. No way she'll actually make it to the top, but there'll be a comfy place for her in one of the lesser circles. I hate that glass ceilings are still a thing, but count me out if getting ahead means emulating her.

Something big and dark in my peripheral vision startles me, though I know it's just my monkey brain's primal response to big flying things. A fertiliser drone the size of a tennis court is working its way along crop rows with the precision of a 3D printer, its whirling rotors making a resonating hum I feel in my body. The bees, datalinked via their hive, have all cleared out from that section for now.

Ten minutes later we crest a rise, and I see the campsite, a clearing with tents neatly arranged around the inflatable lab giving it the look of an army field hospital, more so because of the drab photovoltaics forming the outer surfaces. There's a couple of vehicles; Coppick's SUV and another which must belong to the swarm guys. They're set up close to the forest's edge, a dense, straight treeline from when this land was cleared for cropping. It's a wonder those trees aren't gone too. Small mercies.

I grab my pack from the tray, and Jonas is off, back to his routine. Pick this up, put that there, spray stuff around. Drones do most of the heavy work now, but there's always gaps left for people to fill, especially those that don't ask tough questions.

In the cool of the lab, Coppick and three others stand around a trestle table looking at screens. I recognise Hartley, the guy driving the hardware, but not the other two. Everyone looks up as I enter.

"Ah, Paola, sorry to call you in from days off," says my boss.

"No problem, professor," I say. To be honest, it was touch and go whether I was coming back at all, but she doesn't know that. The department and I have been moving in different philosophical directions for some time.

She introduces me to Xanthe and Christian, datalinking and control experts. I'm covering the ecological side in support of Coppick, who has overall command. She gets straight to the point.

"You know some of this already, but to get us all on the same page, here's the summary. For about two months now, telemetry intercepts from local bee populations have shown anomalies, barely significant in isolation but collectively different enough from projections to be concerning. We're talking about unexpected spread patterns, deviation from optimal work schedules, and in some cases, unexplained total absences. Some divergence is obviously to be expected, but it's the unpredictability that's raising high-level questions."

She double-taps one of the screens, bringing up a magnified view of the fifty square kilometres around us. Overlays show predicted hive coverage against actual, and I'm surprised at the extent of the mismatch. There were signs a week ago when I went on leave, but this is something else. Coppick continues:

"On top of all that, we're seeing behavioural changes, some subtle, others not so much."

That's a hell of an understatement. What very few people except us know is that, two days ago and three kilometres east of here, on the other side of this forest strip, a farm worker died in very unusual circumstances.

Coppick gestures to Hartley, who brings up images on screen. There's a six-wheel ATV with crumpled spray gear upside down in a gully with a man's body laid out a few metres away.

"The driver was in the vehicle when it rolled," Coppick says. "The property manager found him when he didn't return on schedule. Once he'd confirmed the driver was dead, he took these pictures and contacted us."

Close-up shots of the man show bruises and scrapes consistent with what you'd expect from a rollover, but his skin is also peppered with red marks, some still bleeding, as if he's been blasted with buckshot at close range. The vehicle, too, has multiple dents like it's taken numerous hits from small, fast-moving objects.

"And the manager's keeping quiet?" I ask.

"For the moment, which is why we need to move fast," says Coppick.

. . .

Early next morning, Coppick, Christian, and I are moving single-file through the eucalyptus forest, quietly following an animal path in the general direction of our destination waypoint.

Theoretically, the bees should treat us as inconsequential, like anything not directly affecting their work around the crops, but something big's afoot, I know it. Since their real counterparts left us, struck down by flamefronts of disease, these artificial substitutes have filled the pollination gap for critical monoculture crops. We'd already been pushing research in that direction, knowing a crisis had to be coming soon. Military drone swarm and nanobot technology, reluctantly shared by Defence, once orders came down from high enough, allowed us to get them out here quickly. Now, as always when humans muck with nature on a large scale, we're seeing unintended consequences.

The trees thin out ahead and there, gleaming silver-bronze in the middle of a clearing, is the hive. A few bees are circling around, nosing in and out of gum blossoms, but most of them should already be out on task after charging overnight.

"Look at the shape," I whisper. The hive structure, originally cuboid, now has projections and hollows, like a sculptor's been at it with power tools. The fabricator caste have clearly been busy.

"I see it," replies Coppick. "And it's bigger, I'm sure."

"What are they up to, do you think?" Christian asks.

"They have power and raw materials," I say. "We gave them directives, they've taken it from there. But where are they going with this, I wonder?"

Bees glint and fade as they drift in and out of morning shadows. One in particular catches my eye. I point it out to Coppick and she nods.

"See if you can get it," she says.

I slip off my day pack and take out the specimen jar, waiting for the bee to land somewhere low enough. It seems to be ignoring the flowers and instead moving from one vantage point to another. Like a guard would.

They have a small blind spot directly behind, and I'm soon able to trap it in the jar. It doesn't seem fazed, and sits quietly while I carry it back to my companions. I see right away it's quite different from the original specification, bulkier in the body and with a pointed extrusion below the optical sensors, which is what caught my attention in the first place. Coppick's taking close-up images when Christian speaks up.

"Hey, sorry to interrupt, but I think there's something going on over here."

He points to a tree trunk near the hive, where a group of bees has gathered. I can't be sure from this distance, but it looks as if at least some are modified versions like our friend in the jar.

As we step out for a closer look, the bees get airborne and hover near the tree in a close, regular formation. I've almost come to think of them as living creatures, but this is what military drones might do. I'm not sure what's happening, but it doesn't look welcoming.

"Come on," I say, reaching down for my gear and backing away toward the treeline. As the others follow, the bees respond, widening out their spacing and moving nearer to us. Christian's last in line as we turn to beat a hasty retreat, and I hear him yell. Glancing behind, I see a squadron of metallic specks darting down, smacking into his back with enough force to make him stagger. He passes me in a sprint and I'm running too, feeling a sharp impact on my shoulder blade as I dodge trees. At some point I realise they're no longer following us and I stop, holding onto a sapling and dragging in great heaving breaths as I wait for my heart to quit thumping.

. . .

My shoulder's sore enough, but Christian's back is a real mess. Coppick inspects the bloodstained holes in his shirt, while Hartley dabs antiseptic on his wounds.

"At least these aren't too deep," Hartley says.

"I'm sure they weren't going easy on us, though," I say, thinking of the pictures of the dead man. "We were just lucky they didn't have room to get up to full speed, and we got away quick enough for them to figure we weren't a threat any more."

"But a soldier caste!" says Coppick. "That wasn't an original directive, and there are no natural predators, of course. It doesn't fit with any simulations I'm aware of. We're going to have to put a lid on this, quickly."

I'm not certain what she means by that, but it worries me.

She turns to Xanthe, who's working at a terminal.

"What have you been seeing in telemetry?" she asks.

Xanthe pulls up graphics and arranges them across the screens, showing what's been coming in from the hives and tracking stations. There's the usual concentration around this forest's two hives, but distinct lobes lead off in unexpected directions.

"What are those?" I ask, pointing.

"Not really sure," says Xanthe. "I thought they were just random at first, but as the picture builds, it's looking like they're establishing new corridors."

"To where, though?" I wonder aloud. "What's out there?"

She overlays a vegetation map and zooms in. The new routes correspond to concentrations of flowering trees and shrubs, so it looks to me as if the bees have set themselves a new program.

"What about the reporting?" I ask.

"Data streams are getting patchier all the time, although they're clearly still transmitting. It's just not in the right format."

So they're still talking—just not to us.

. . .

It's getting towards sunset, and Hartley and I have gone out for a smoke. The heat's gone out of the day, and there's hardly any wind. Reminds me of camping as a kid, an idyllic setting, but I can't relax.

"There's something I feel like I should be seeing, but it's not coming to me," I say.

Hartley slaps at a mosquito.

"I wish it was these bastards that died out, not the bees," he says.

"They've got their place too, and we probably only know the half of it," I reply. "The problem with ecosystems is, you start fiddling with one thing and three others go haywire."

"Can't you just do some kind of reset on the bees?"

He's a good technician, but he doesn't have the big picture.

"If we could, that'd be great. Thing is, we don't actually control them, there's too many variables. We'd fail dismally if we tried. Essentially we've set them a job—to pollinate—and given them a toolbox. In biological terms, they're simply evolving. To change them, we'd have to kill them."

"So what are they thinking? What's their plan?"

"They don't have a plan as such. We're not talking about a thinking mind making reasoned decisions here, any more than a hive of real bees could. Looks like their scope has widened from just crops to plants in general, and honestly, I don't think that's a bad thing."

"But if they're turning on us, what's *our* next step?"

I take a long drag and exhale into the gathering darkness.

"That's the big question, my friend."

. . .

Coppick and I are in the lab before sunrise next day. The bee I caught yesterday is still in its jar prison on the table, low on charge and moving sluggishly. My boss is on the phone, her subservient tone showing it's the department head or higher she's talking to. Her voice is low but it's not hard to get the gist—neutralise the threat, blast radius, authorisation, press statements. When she's done I can't contain myself.

"You're going to destroy the hives? Just like that?"

She looks at me like we're meeting for the first time and she doesn't like what she sees.

"You have any real alternatives, doctor?"

"You call this a real alternative? All you're doing is kicking the problem down the road. What are you going to do next year? Pollinate by hand? Or deploy more bees and expect a different outcome from doing the same

62

thing? I'm sorry, I've already seen one mass extinction, and I'm not going to be party to another."

"Get out," she says. "Get the others in here, but don't bother coming back yourself."

She turns her back and punches her call button again.

I bite back my anger and storm out. While I'm deciding whether to do as she says or not, a vehicle approaches, kicking up dust. It's the manager, looking agitated.

"You guys transmitting anything on the drone band here?" he demands.

"No, we've only got receivers, apart from phones," I say. "Why, what's the matter?"

"Machinery's acting up, tractors and such. It's not mechanical. They're running all right, just not doing what they're supposed to."

Roused by the noise, the others are emerging from their tents.

I'm putting pieces together in my mind. Real bees ensure the continuation of plant species over generations. Ours exist for the same reason, but go about it differently. If a threat is detected, it needs to be countered, and here, the biggest threat is *us*.

I become aware of a hum, felt more than heard. Then it grows to a metallic scream as labouring motors go far beyond limits, and I see the giant spray drone rise high above the treeline, tilting and swaying.

"Run!" I shout. We scatter like ants as it comes angling down, gathering speed on a collision course with the lab.

###

About the Author

Tim Borella is an Australian author, mainly of short speculative fiction published in anthologies, online and in podcasts. He is a regular contributor to the *Antipodean SF* online magazine, and placed third and second, respectively, in the 2020 and 2021 Australian Natcon Conflux short story competitions. Recent short story publications include "Tox Hunt," in the *Stories of Survival* anthology (Deadset Press 2021), "The Talbotville Centaur," in the *Sagittarius* anthology (Deadset Press 2021), and "Miss Deborah," in the *Haunted* anthology (Specul8 Publishing 2021).

He's also a songwriter, and is fortunate to have spent most of his working life doing something else he loves, flying. Tim lives with his wife Georgie in North Queensland, in an area recognised as the traditional lands of the Ngadjon-jii people. More information is available on his Tim Borella – Author Facebook page.

*****~~~~~*****

Showdown at Sueño Hueco

by Wulf Moon

It's bloody hard work being a lawman. My samurai ancestors knew that, chasing deadly bandits into forests, facing down outlaws with skills as good as their own. Life and death balanced daily on the razor-sharp edge of a *katana*, and the samurai stayed alive by keeping their bodies in tonal balance, and their minds as sharp as their swords.

Out here under the baleful eye of Proxima Centauri, we don't have forests. Hell, the terrain I'm gunning my knobby-tired electric Z-chopper over looks like rolling hills of pottery shards. But they say we'll make Proxima b green one day—solar winds are nasty here, but they haven't blown the ozone away thanks to the strong magnetic field. Lots of towns get seeded over new reservoir and mineral discoveries, and enterprising settlers and industries sprout up with each new claim. It's the Wild West out here, only the West is 4.243 light years from where she used to be. You can't breathe the atmosphere.

And it's colder, minus thirty Celsius most times. People say when hell freezes over? They mean Proxima b.

I'm dropping down a decline heading for the gulch of Sueño Hueco, a Hispanic outpost. No law against trying to preserve your culture. Hell, my whole life has been trying to uphold my own culture that's been almost forgotten. There are laws, however, about decapitating colonists, and I've got a crime scene called in. Call was garbled—damn these solar flares—but I made out the name of the town, and here I am. A lot of crimes go unreported in the back of beyond, and when you ask about the missing, nine times outta ten you're told they're out prospecting. Funny how many dead prospectors I've found that took the time to bury themselves under Proxima's shards before breathing their last. Like I said, Wild West.

I pull up to the biodome entrance and kill the engine. Terracotta-colored girders with clear hexagonal panels span the dome. Big sucker, like six football stadiums. I tap the wrist display on my suit. Talismán Biotech. Not a mining venture then. This one's a bioengineering research facility, and the director is an astrobiologist: Dr. Isabella Astuto.

Time to meet the locals.

My headlamp is a drone, closest thing I have to a partner. I chose her specs, intuitive AI, feminine persona. Hey, it gets lonely on the trail. Sweet voice, but she's got pipes that can stun a helmeted prospector in their tracks. I call her Gunpowder.

"Hey, Gunpowder."

I watch her unclamp and hover in the air, chrome-silver shiny. Her cyclops eye is on the metal base below the headlamp, but she communicates through my tympanic earplant. "Hey, Takeo. Ready for another day of adventure?"

"My own personal *Jupiter's Travels*."

"'Reader Beware: Because of this book men and women have been known to leave their jobs and take to the road. In fifteen years it has changed many lives. It could change yours.'"

"Ain't that the truth. All I've ever wanted was to ride to the edge of the world and see what lies beyond."

"Mission accomplished?"

"Ride ain't over yet, sweetie. Go ring the doorbell, will ya?"

"*Ding-dong.*" She flies off and hovers before the door with its own cyclops eye. "This is the police. Open in the name of the Proxima Alliance Marshals, or we'll break this door down!"

I chuckle as I dismount and back the bike onto its kickstand. "Easy, Gunpowder."

"That was just for you. How's my humor coming along?"

"Don't quit your day job."

"Awww."

"You done good, you heard me laugh. Now what's the hold-up? They have to know we're here. Flash the badge."

Blue light shines from her eye into the door's optics. As Gunpowder deals with security, I disconnect my burgundy-colored armored suit from the bike's air tank. The controls switch to the auxilliary on my backpack. I wish I could leave my brain bucket on the bike handles like they did in the old days, but I need the scanners in the helm for crime scenes. Besides, can't breathe this soupy atmosphere. Yet.

I stride toward the facility's double doors. Where the hell is their doorman?

"Anything?"

Gunpowder spins about. "Still on hold. I'm listening to a moving passage of 'El Condor Pasa.'"

"I hate waiting. Pop it."

"As you wish." Gunpowder launches the security override. "Tracking its circuits, almost there. Want me for backup?"

"No, O2's low on the bike. Rustle up a fill from their electrolysis station's bots. Make sure we get charged the Alliance Marshals' discount."

"Affirmative."

"And guard the bike. Don't need a scav pretending it's been abandoned."

"Got it."

I hear the door click through the helmet's audio.

"There we are," Gunpowder says.

The airlock opens with a serpent's hiss.

. . .

I'm in the outer rim of the facility, a curved hallway with offices along the exterior wall. My faceplate readouts say I've got breathable air, so I retract the helm. The articulated plates slide out to each side, looking much like the *shikoro* on a samurai's helmet. I know the *katana* swinging on my left hip finishes the look. Might not clear regs on Earth, but this ain't homeworld. I take a deep breath. Place is hot and steamy, smells like decayed eggs. Sulphur.

My footsteps echo around me, like I'm being followed. Where are the people? Overheads wink on as I pass under them, buzzing like bees, banishing the shadows, but the offices are empty and dark. One door says "Security," so I poke my head in. Dark as hell, but I hear faint gasps, like someone's on a respirator, and in the shadows—

Damn! A skull pops in front of my face! All blue turquoise with sockets rimmed in black, blood-red glowing eyes, and a ghoulish grin that says, "I'm short on brains and yours look delicious." My adrenaline surges. I jump back, drop my hand to the braided handle of my sword hilt. . . and let go. Hell, it's just an android, painted up like a creepy skeleton, moving its jaw to simulate speech.

"You are not authorized to be here," the skeleton says in the worst "Mean Robot" I've ever heard. "Intruder!"

My breastplate has all kinds of compartments and tricks. I tap it, and the fiber optics light up: *P.A. Marshal*, complete with name and badge number. I can see those red brands in the android's sockets dull a shade. Message received.

"State your business, Marshal Koiguchi."

"Dr. Isabella Astuto. Where is she?"

The skeleton-painted android steps into the hallway. "It's a holiday. *Dia de los Muertos*. Day of the Dead. The staff are celebrating in the arboretum. They are not to be disturbed."

I strike my authority pose, hands on hips. "And I was told there's a dead body. Take me to the director."

Skeleton-head's eyes glow like fire and brimstone when I mention a body. "Reach for the sky, lawman! This is the private property of Talismán Biotech. Proceed immediately to the exit or I shall escort you from the premises."

"Hey, buddy, official business. Law says I can have a look around."

"You were warned." The android drops a firm hand on my shoulder and shoves me back.

If there's one law on Earth or Proxima, it's if you assault an officer, you suffer the consequences. In one fluid motion I glide the blade from its *saya*, activate the molecular disruptor along its edge, lift it to my right, and with two hands firmly on the handle I swing down in an arc across the android's neck. Its head severs clean from its frame and clanks against the floor. The wiring in its neck sparks as blue oil spurts into the air. The body drops, quivering. I shake its oil from the blade in the *chiburui* move, then return the *katana* to its *saya*.

The skull clacks its jaw, working up and down in a puddle of fluids. I wish the lights in its eyes would go out. Its polymer lips are still curled in that rictus grin.

"Enjoy the party," the severed head says, laughing hysterically.

I give the head a kick. It clatters down the hall, cackling all the way.

"*Sayonara.*"

There's no security eye and no leering robot blocking the arboretum portal. It opens like a camera iris, and that rotten egg steam instantly washes over me. Geothermal. Night has fallen, but there's glowing fireflies everywhere the size of hornets, lighting tendrils of mist that meander through what I can only describe as a recreated Amazonian jungle.

A ramp leads down to the jungle floor, vines entwining its sides and arching overhead like a covered bridge. I blink my eyes, thinking it's a trick of the mists, but creepers and lianas continue rolling over and under one another like a bed of snakes. I hear atonal music playing deep within the jungle, and voices too, of women chanting. There are broad-leafed plants, bushes, and tropical trees everywhere, but I see a path leading toward the center of the arboretum. In that center is by far the most amazing thing I've seen on this world: a tree rising up at least seventy meters, branches fanning out like deformed limbs. As I take in a canopy that spreads from one end of the dome to the other, I recall the legendary trees of Japanese folklore.

I descend the bridge to the world below, creepers wriggling out from under my feet. I am reminded again of my ancestors, chasing deadly bandits into the woods. Out here under the baleful eye of Proxima Centauri, it appears we *do* have forests.

. . .

The Great Tree. That's all I can call it. I enter the clearing where its roots rise up like buttresses on a gnarled and twisted tower. Crimson hibiscus-looking flowers cover its trunk and branches, but they are clever camouflage for wicked thorns lurking beneath. One of the curving trunk buttresses provides the backdrop for a banquet table, and the music in the air stops, as if I stumbled upon a secret gathering of spirits. Perhaps I have, for the thirteen beings around the table are draped in white gossamer. I am reminded of the *kodama*, ancient tree spirits of Japan.

One rises, throws back her cowl, and moves toward me, a sphere of fireflies following her as a glow-globe. She has mahogany-colored skin and obsidian black hair that cascades down her shoulders. The cloying mists covering the ground swirl as she steps, and the fabric draping her could just as easily have been spun from mists—it's so sheer, nothing is left to the imagination. But it's her eyes that bewitch me, for in spite of my armored suit, I feel as naked as a newborn as I stare into them.

Her lips move, but they are whispers blown over the whorls of my ears. "Who are you, stranger? How did you bypass my security?"

Security? Recalling that maniacal head rolling down the hallway shakes me from her spell. I note the others sitting around a table lit with silver candelabra and gaudily painted skulls. Hispanic women, eyeing me like wolves chancing upon a lamb. If this is a feast, why are there only ceramic knives on the table? Weird. I look back to their leader, tap my breastplate. My ID lights up.

I honor her with the *keirei* bow. "Takeo Koiguchi, P.A. Marshal. Are you Dr. Isabella Astuto?"

She gives the nod of one dealing with an inferior. "Why are you here?"

Isabella's gaze unnerves me. I look down. "We received a garbled report that traced back to this facility. Female, says she found her husband decapitated, send help. Ring any bells?"

71

Isabella touches my chin and lifts my head. I'm drawn into those dark depths again as mirthful laughter spills from her lips. "My dear lawman, that was Maria, hosting a Day of the Dead reading last night over the com system. Part of our festivities. She must have pushed the wrong button."

"A wrong button that transmitted direct to the district marshals' dispatcher?"

She traces my lips with a fingertip. So incredibly soft. I back a step, breaking contact. Lick my lips. Tastes sweet, like a melange of cinnamon and sugar and nutmeg.

"My dear, dear marshal. We are on Proxima. Stranger things have happened."

I take a deep breath, about to cite an ordinance that allows me to search the premises. Starlight sparkles in the pools of her eyes. I could swim in those pools. Why did I think they were cold and calculating? Why was I bothering this gorgeous lady? I was the intruder here. I had interrupted their celebration. Shame flushes my cheeks.

"I am so sorry to have disturbed you, mistress." I have disrupted *wa*, their communal harmony. I bow my deepest and count to three. "Please forgive my callous intrusion."

That lightest laughter again, the sound of wind chimes swirling through my mind. "Think nothing of it, *Takeo*." She glides her finger along the exposed portion of my throat. Her voice purrs deep as a panther's. "Take the suit off and join us. We would enjoy male company tonight."

Something at the base of my skull cries out, but it's a cricket chirp in the fog.

Her fingertip rises up, touching the soft flesh behind my earlobe, igniting desire. She leans in. "*Take it off.*"

The cricket chirps louder. My suit is my armor. Armor saves my life.

The Voice. "Wouldn't it feel delicious to strip naked in the mist and dance with me under the fireflies?"

It's been long since I've been with a woman. She smells like cinnamon. I taste warm apple pie in my mouth, the supple sugary glaze dripping on my palate. I'm hungry. Starving. That cricket doesn't stand a chance. I lower my gaze to the breastplate's release.

My *katana*! It's gone. That cricket is screaming like a siren at a five alarm fire. I jump back from Isabella and the fog rolls from my mind.

She has my sword. She slides the blade from its sheath, screams, hurls it into the brush. "You dare bring forged steel before the Sacred Ceiba? The World Tree guarded by the spirit of Xtabay? You could have destroyed all we've worked to achieve!"

I note the area where my blade landed. I'm out of her spell, and I'm thinking that dance is off. But I feel more naked than ever I did before. I place my left foot forward, slide my right back, ready to lunge. "Look, lady. I don't know what kind of research facility you're running, and I haven't a clue who Ceiba and this Ish-Tabay is. I've got a distress call, possible crime. I'm going to have a look around."

Those eyes like glittering pools? They're bubbling tar pits now.

"I was afraid you'd say that." Isabella lifts that delicate hand and flicks her finger. A glowing hornet zips from the hovering glow-globe, striking fire into my neck.

As I fall to the ground, I hear that cricket playing his little song. *Told you so.*

. . .

I dream of a Tree with roots burrowing the depths of the underworld, a trunk standing tall in the world of men, and branches that span from star to star. The vision fades; my eyelids crack open. Shadows. Cold. Pressure bearing down on my chest. Hard to breathe. I tilt my head in the faint light and see roots constricting around my

73

torso and neck. They can't choke me entirely, for even pulled back, the articulated plating of my helm offers some protection. But tendrils that smell of humus are probing my nostrils and worming in my ears and fingering my eyelids like a buyer inspecting bluefin tuna at a Tokyo fish market.

That clears my head. I jerk upright. I'm in a crevice below one of those buttress roots, with the animated tree testing my every crack. I can move a little, the roots slithering across my armor, seeking the release. Good luck with that.

My helm's feeds are always on, boosting the signal from my tympanic implant. I call my partner. "Gunpowder!"

Nothing. Damn biodome must be shielded, and that raises red flags. What's their secret? Narcotics lab?

Laughter falls like echoes in a forest. Light shines from above. I shift about. See up through the crevice. Isabella stares down, the glowing hornets behind her head forming a wicked nimbus.

"Foolish men. It takes so little to control you. I did not need my drugs. You would have fallen to desire."

"Like hell." I shudder as a hissing tendril writhes past my lips. I spit it out. "Why are you feeding me to a tree?" I struggle against its bonds. "What. . . the hell. . . is. . . this thing?"

Isabella flourishes her arms toward the tree's limbs. "My life's work, the study of the Sacred Cieba. My ancestors worshipped this tree. The goddess Xtabay tested men beneath its boughs. Those that failed—like you— were fed to the roots of the World Tree."

I push my right hand against the roots, working it slowly across my torso. "So this tree is some freaked out genetic modification?"

"Our specialty at Talismán Biotech. This cieba will bless its worshippers. It has been bioengineered to increase oxygen production by a factor of ten through accelerated respiration. But the modified chlorophyll requires a boost of soluble heme iron as its catalyst, and hemoglobin is the perfect source."

"Blood? Human blood?"

"Xtabay demands it. She has always fed from the blood of *men*." Isabella rests her hands on her hips. "My associates are distributing seedlings to other habitats, certified by our phytologists, hailed as an oxygenating revolution. On a world without breathable atmosphere, our trees that accelerate oxygen production will become the new gold—oxygen free from the expense of the electrolysis process! Colonists will plant them in their biodomes. . . and through them, my people will propagate our ancestral religion."

I keep working my hand to my left. Almost there. "I call it a cult."

She points down at me. The gossamer fabric sways around her curves, but it's lost all its charm. "I call it Proxima's future."

"Not if I can help it." I've lost my *katana*. True. But a samurai carries two swords. I hide my *wakizashi* in a sealed compartment on the left side of my breastplate. It snicks open to my touch.

I grip the hilt of the short blade. Slide it out. Slash.

I've never heard a tree scream before.

The scream grows into a roar, as I rip my blade across the tendrils choking my face. I smell iron. I move to cut away the ones around my torso, but they are already flailing in retreat.

Isabella adds her screams as the ground shudders. "What are you doing? You beast! You're damaging her!"

I fight to stand and look up. The ground continues to quake. Isabella cries out, as she totters backward. Her glowing ball of hornets scatters.

Not a long climb up this crevice, maybe five meters to the surface. A root snaps out and lashes me in the face. Bitch. Knows right where my armor doesn't cover.

Well, two can play that game. I plunge my blade deep into her pulpy taproot. Another scream stuns me for a moment. That cricket at the base of my skull? He's singing *climb, baby, climb.*

. . .

When you fight hand to hand, it's all a blur, it's moving so fast. With multiple combatants, you strike to bleed out, weaken your opponents, there's no time to kill. But I get in a clean slice across Isabella's throat while she's wailing in shock over her shuddering tree. That leaves twelve.

There's too many to fight my way back to where I lost my *katana*. I back toward a buttress root, protecting my rear, and the women advance. Feet and fists and ceramic knives flash in blurred fury. My counters are automatic, more muscle memory than conscious thought. These witches—I mean botanists—have skills, and my adrenaline surges as I block and strike.

A side kick exposes a thigh; I slash across it with my blade and the assailant drops, femoral artery bleeding out. My opening. I leap over her body and run for the bridge. I don't hear footsteps following. You cross blades with a samurai marshal, you think twice before doing it again.

I reach the ramp out of the jungle, and my spirits soar.

Vegetation shudders.

The damned skeleton-droid jumps out of the bushes, holding its head up to see. Wireless optical? I don't know, but I leap past, and it chases me up that ramp. A vine snakes out, and I trip and slam against the diamond plate and see stars. Dammit. At least I took a few with me.

. . .

But I've got a partner. She's a hellcat when it comes to protecting me. Thank the gods she checks the comm when she decides I'm taking too long and gets no response. She buzzes in, I know her whir. She bellows, "STOP in the name of the law," and I lift my head up to see her slam smack into that android's skull. The head goes flying like a line drive at a ball game. If that place had been a stadium, the crowds would be roaring.

I call in more marshals before going back in. *Okaasan* didn't raise no fool.

Four women dead, including one Dr. Isabella Astuto. Nine missing. We find a hidden evac tunnel. Blood everywhere. We take out that tree. Find the men's desiccated bodies, too, wrapped in its roots. We shut that place down. Perma-seal the doors and post Colonial X13 Guardian drones. No one's getting past them.

I'm straddling my bike again, *katana* recovered, sheathed at my side. Work's over at Sueño Hueco. Last man standing. Closest I've come to riding to the edge and seeing what lies beyond.

Gunpowder locks into position. "Hey, Takeo. Ready for another day of adventure?"

"My own personal *Jupiter's Travels*."

"Where to?"

I breathe in. Release a cleansing sigh. "Gotta hunt down those mad scientists that went into the nursery business."

"Affirmative. Keep the rubber side down."

I plant my left foot out and lean into a spin turn, rear tire spitting up gravel. "Always."

It's bloody hard work being a lawman. Like I said, *Wild* West.

About the Author

Wulf Moon lives with his wife and their seven sinister cats on the Olympic Peninsula of Washington

State. He wrote his first science fiction story when he was fifteen. It won the national Scholastic Art & Writing Awards, and became his first pro sale in *Science World.*

Moon's stories have appeared in numerous publications, including *Writers of the Future, Best of Deep Magic Anthology Two, Star Trek: Strange New Worlds 2* by Pocket Books, *Galaxy's Edge, DreamForge,* and *Best of Third Flatiron.* He is podcast director at *Future Science Fiction Digest.*

Moon is a writing coach and teaches the Super Secrets of Writing Workshops. He has won Best Author and Best Writing Workshop three years in a row in the Critters Readers Choice Awards. His Super Secrets of Writing books are scheduled for publication this year by Stark Publishing Solutions.

Wulf Moon invites you to friend him on Facebook at wulf.moon.94; follow him on Twitter @WulfMoon1; or join his Wulf Pack at TheSuperSecrets.com.

*****~~~~~*****

PAST DUE

Reassessed Value

by David Hankins

Liam stood in his farmhouse's doorway, gnarled fingers gripping his holstered pulser, and wondered if tax assessors qualified as thieves. The law let him shoot thieves. McConnell Orchards surrounded his farmhouse, one hundred acres that smelled of rotting fruit, moldering leaves, and despair.

The assessor, a mousy little man named Mr. Gage, stood ramrod straight. "Mr. McConnell, as a corporate team member—"

"I am *not* part of Treecorp," Liam growled, voice rough from too many cigars. He thrust a finger at Gage. "McConnells have farmed Tyree for generations! *We* were the first colonists. *We* discovered the Koge!" A bitter native fruit that looked like an orange, but crunched like an apple, the Koge developed unique sugars when grown intertwined with apple trees. Sugars that accelerated the human mind to genius levels.

Gage cleared his throat. "Regardless, you must pay your property taxes. The eminent domain acquired by Treecorp is quite clear."

"Convoluted laws written by crooked lawyers to steal my land."

79

"Based on assessed value, your current tax burden is two hundred seventy thousand—"

"I can't pay that!" Liam shoved past the man and waved at his orchard. Withered Koge intertwined with vibrant green apple trees. "Perhaps you didn't notice, but the Koge trees are all dead. Killed by Treecorp's asinine customs waivers for contaminated goods. Y'all brought the fungal rot in, so y'all can stuff those taxes where the sun don't shine. I got a granddaughter to feed!"

The assessor tapped his tablet. "Very well. I've noted your refusal to pay. Consider this your eviction notice."

The farmhouse's porch suddenly felt too small. Liam's breath came fast and he found his pulser in hand, pointed at the assessor's forehead. He didn't remember drawing it. "You're not taking my land."

Gage's eyes bulged, but he set his jaw. "The law is on my side."

"How's that gonna help you from six feet under?" Liam's finger tightened on the trigger.

"Grandpa?" Clara's voice cut through Liam's fury. The six-year-old stood in the doorway, arms crossed over her coveralls. "Are you a bad person?"

Her words were ice water down Liam's spine. It was the question he asked whenever she misbehaved, to make her think about her actions. Your actions define you. He lowered the pulser and growled at Gage, "Get off my land."

"This is Treecorp property, legally claimed by eminent domain and—"

"Now!" Liam whipped the pistol up, his hand shaking.

The assessor raised his hands and backed off the porch. "You have five days, Mr. McConnell. Pay your taxes, or we *will* evict you."

"You'd better bring an army."

"I will."

The little bureaucrat straightened his suit, spun on his heel, and stormed off.

. . .

Liam had a hard time meeting Clara's gaze as he prepared dinner. The slump to her thin shoulders made acid churn in his stomach. He'd almost murdered a man in front of her. What was wrong with him?

But what could he do? McConnell Orchards was all he had.

For the next five days.

He hadn't complained when Treecorp's money had poured in. Every human in the Federation of Planets wanted the Koge. It gave the ultimate caffeine high, was worth billions, but only grew on the planet of Tyree. Then two years of viral fungal rot had wiped out the Koge, sending the ecosystem and the economy into a death spiral. Liam had stretched his money, saved his apple trees—they'd been bred for hardiness—but their intertwined Koge had all died.

Meager apple sales had kept McConnell Orchards afloat. Barely.

Liam wrangled his spiraling thoughts and glared at the beans in his pot. Beans and apples were all he had left. He scooped dinner onto two plates, giving Clara the greater portion. She was getting too skinny.

"Grandpa?"

"What's on your mind, Sweetie?"

"Two questions." That pulled a smile from Liam. She was too smart for her age. Just like her mother had been, before the accident. "What's eminent domain?"

Liam's smile dropped. "That's lawyer-speak for stealing yer land, legal-like 'for the greater good.'" He snarled that last bit.

She nodded like he'd confirmed her guess. "If it's legal, don't we have to do what that man said? You always say to do what's right, no matter what."

Liam gazed into Clara's worried green eyes. How to explain this? "Just because something's legal, don't mean it's right. Land values and taxes skyrocketed with the value of the Koge. Then the economy collapsed, leaving everyone with bills and taxes they can't pay. Treecorp doesn't care. Every credit they pull out of me is one less they have to pay to *their* debtors. It's legal, but it ain't right." He paused for another question, Clara always had more questions, but she just nodded and started in on her beans.

Hours later, Liam sat slumped on his porch swing, alone in the dark. A glowing cigar dangled in one hand, a whiskey tumbler in the other. Rockets rumbled skyward in the distance beyond Treecorp's factory and company town. Evacuation arks loaded with everything of value as the corporation drained every last cent from the economy.

Corporate bastards.

Liam pulled on his cigar, held the harsh smoke, then exhaled. Where the hell would he find a quarter million credits in five days? He had no family beyond Clara. No wealthy in-laws or dowager aunts. The neighbors were just as desperate, each within months of penury, eviction, and starvation. Did anybody off-planet know what was happening on Tyree? Did they care?

That thought gave Liam pause. The Federation was a loose coalition of planets, but they had ultimate legal authority. It tore at Liam's very soul to beg for help, but today's brush with murder had shaken him. He dug out his commlink and threw up the holo-display.

Thirty minutes later, he'd found the Federation Office of Citizen Advocates. An hour after that, he'd navigated the automated process and reached an actual advocate. Interstellar video calls were ridiculously expensive, but what was one more bill added to the stack? A well-coiffed woman identified herself as Barrister Strickland, and he grimaced. Another lawyer. Liam swallowed his pride and explained his situation. The lawyer was unfazed.

"You're calling because you don't want to pay your taxes?" she said.

"No, the taxes are wrong."

"I'm looking at your file and I assure you, the numbers are accurate."

"They need to reassess my land. It's not worth what they say it is. Nothing on Tyree is."

"Ah, I see. Citizens in good standing can request a value reassessment at any time—"

"Thank God!"

"—but the key words here are 'in good standing.' You cannot request a reassessment until your current tax burden is paid."

Liam's whiskey curdled in his stomach. "You. . . you're not going to help?"

"I'm sorry, but it's the law."

But it wasn't right.

Liam screamed and threw his commlink into the darkness. It spun end over end, holo-screen flashing in a spiral before it bounced off a dead Koge tree with a crack of plastic. His hands shook with fury and frustration.

No one cared. No one would help.

He was going to lose everything.

. . .

Sunrise found Liam lying awake in bed. Dishes clattered in the kitchen as Clara looked for breakfast. She was a good kid. Crazy independent, like all McConnells.

A familiar knot formed in Liam's throat as Clara sang off-key. Her mother Abigail, Liam's daughter, had done the same when she cooked. Abigail had died a few years back when her land-speeder crashed into a Treecorp heavy hauler. Liam blamed bad weather on dirt roads, but the lawyers had blamed Abigail. They'd handed Liam a bill for damages at her funeral.

The sound of a crashing plate sent Liam scrambling for the stairs.

In the kitchen, he found Clara standing over shattered ceramic and spilled apple slices sprinkled with the last of their sugar. She'd used a kitchen knife without him? Tears welled in Clara's eyes when she saw him and words gushed out.

"I made you a treat cuz you were so sad, but I tripped and broke your favorite plate and I'm sorrrrrrry Grandpa!" Tears poured out and Liam knelt, pulling Clara into his arms. He glanced at the plate. It was one Abigail had made, painted as a school project when she was a kid.

"Shush, now. It's okay." He squeezed Clara. Little nails dug into his back as hot tears soaked his shirt. Liam's heart ached and he held on just as fiercely. "Are you hurt?" he asked and got a vigorous headshake against his chest. "Are you worried about losing our home?"

Pause, squeeze, and the tiniest head nod.

"Me too. But we're not licked yet. We're McConnells. We'll think of something."

Clara's muffled voice spoke into his chest. "What 'bout the apples?"

"They're not worth enough to pay Treecorp's taxes."

She pulled back and turned serious eyes on him. "I could sell my toys. I don't need them any more. I'm a big girl. You say so all the time."

Liam's heart broke and he pulled her back in so she wouldn't see his threatening tears. Grandfathers do *not* cry.

"I'll take care of it, Sweetie. I promise." He squeezed Clara again, kissed her tousled head, then stood. "Now, about this plate."

Clara hunched in on herself.

"It can't be unbroken," he said, "but perhaps you can make it into something new. Something better."

She gave him a confused look.

84

Reassessed Value

"I always liked this plate, it makes me think of your Mama. Why don't you use your fancy colored glues to make something that'll make me think of her *and* you? We can hang it over the mantle."

Clara's eyes lit up and she scrambled up the stairs to her room for her craft bin.

Liam set to cleaning up and made breakfast. Clara returned and sat at the table with intense focus, reassembling the plate with sparkle-infused glues. It would be a disaster when she finished, but Liam knew he'd love it.

Heaviness settled over Liam as he boiled beans for breakfast. He had to save McConnell Orchards. For Clara. He'd promised.

But how?

He had four days.

. . .

Liam spent the day traveling to neighboring farms with Clara, hoping to sell his tractors. Everyone sympathized, but nobody had money to spare. Worst off were those closest to the company town. Tyree's unemployed population had turned hungry, desperate, and larcenous. Liam helped secure barns and equipment wherever he visited, despite his dwindling time.

He called more distant farms as he drove around, but with the same results. He tried the bank, who knew his number, but they declined his call.

No surprise there.

One neighbor gave him a tip about an off-planet market for Koge wood. But the guy's contact only made empty promises of future sales. Call back in four weeks.

Liam didn't have four weeks.

The day ended with him slouched on his porch again, smoking a cigar, and watching Treecorp's silver evacuation ships depart. It was like watching his dreams sail away, never to return.

. . .

A crash from the barn propelled Liam out of bed. He swept the curtains aside and peered into the darkness. He didn't see anything but knew that thieves had come for what little he had left.

Not today.

Liam threw on a bathrobe, grabbed his pulser and a flashlight, and bolted into the chilly darkness.

He stormed into the barn, bathrobe flaring. His pulser and flashlight found a gaunt young man who clutched a bag of beans like a shield. The thief's ragged suit and loafers looked like they'd been expensive once.

Liam snarled. This problem he could handle.

"Whaddya value? Them beans, or your life?" Liam said.

The thief dropped the bag and gulped. Then he shook himself, straightened, and extended a hand. "I think we got off on the wrong foot. Marken Dobbs, former Treecorp lawyer, currently seeking employment."

Liam spat to one side. *Lawyers.* "You shoulda left on Treecorp's fancy evacuation ships."

Marken grimaced, hand dropping. "My contract had an abandonment clause 'in the event of catastrophic crop failure.' Termination without transportation rights. I never expected they'd actually use it."

"Seem kinda stupid for a lawyer."

"Maybe. But the signing bonus was. . . significant. Then the Koge died, the layoffs began, and now I'm stealing beans."

"Tyree's gold rush ended, and we're paying the price." Liam's lips pursed. "It ain't right. Assessor's demanding ruinous property taxes of me, assessed *before* the Koge died."

"Taxation under Treecorp's charter is fairly straightforward." The lawyer cocked an eyebrow as if surprised that Liam *hadn't* paid.

"You got a quarter-million credits in yer back pocket?"

"Uh, no." Marken pointed nervously at the pulser. "Would you mind lowering that?"

Liam ignored him, years of frustration pouring out. "Treecorp stole my land in the name of eminent domain and now they want to steal it again!"

"It's not theft. It's the law."

"It ain't right!" Liam's finger tightened on the trigger.

"But there's a loophole."

Heart racing, Liam pulled himself back from the edge of violence. "What kind?"

"Give me one solid meal, and I'll show you."

"I can shoot you now, and for once the law is on my side."

"Or you could save your land. Your home."

That put a lump in Liam's throat, but he ground his teeth. "I ain't taking the word of a lawyer. Show me the loophole, then we'll talk."

Marken eyed the unwavering pulser and retrieved a communicator. He threw up a holo-display of the Treecorp charter. "Here, see? Treecorp's eminent domain only applies to 'lands bearing Koge trees.' Get rid of the trees and they lose jurisdiction."

"But the Koge are intertwined with my apple trees. I can't destroy one without losing the other."

"That's your choice, but you'd be free of the corporation."

Liam chewed on his lip. Could he destroy everything on the word of a lawyer and a thief? How would he feed Clara? An image flashed in his mind of the plate Clara had broken. He'd felt like that plate for a long time—broken without hope of repair. These orchards were all he knew.

It was time to build something new. Something better.

He had three days. He'd better hurry.

Liam lowered the pulser and pointed with the flashlight. "Grab that fuel line. Should be long enough to soak the first orchard rows. I'll meet you outside in a minute."

"Huh?" Marken's forehead scrunched under his lanky hair.

"We're burning McConnell Orchards to the ground, but I can't raze a hundred acres by myself. Yer hired. Now get to work. I need to make some calls."

. . .

It became known as the Great Fire of Tyree. Convincing the neighbors to torch their orchards wasn't hard once he showed them the loophole. Everyone chafed under Treecorp.

McConnell Orchards was the first in danger of repossession, so the neighbors descended with backhoes, dozers, and tractors. At the end of three days, Liam's land looked like a war zone. Each burned-out husk they'd torn out had wrenched his soul, but they'd done it. Not a single Koge remained.

When Mr. Gage returned, he brought his army of security goons. They flowed out of black corporate landspeeders, weapons low and ready. Liam and Marken waited on the front lawn, arms crossed, while Clara watched wide-eyed from the porch.

The assessor looked around with furious indignation. "You'll go to jail for this!" He whipped out his tablet and started tapping.

Liam drew a deep breath of ash-laden air and nodded to Marken. This had better work.

Marken straightened his still-ragged suit. "This land no longer belongs to Treecorp."

The assessor glanced up. "What are you talking about?"

"Please refer to subchapter seventy-three, paragraph six of the Treecorp charter. Treecorp has eminent domain over all lands containing Koge trees."

The assessor swiped on his tablet to read. "Now, note in paragraph eight that lands found *not* containing Koge trees remain with the original owners." Marken gave the devastated fields an exaggerated examination. "I don't see any Koge trees."

The assessor read, swiped, read some more, then glared. "That won't stand up in court. This is Treecorp property!"

Liam growled, "Not anymore." He withdrew his communicator and threw up the holo-display. Barrister Strickland's severe face gazed out.

"Mr. Gage," she said, "I represent the Federation in matters of citizen advocacy. Initially, I agreed with you, but after further discussion with Mr. McConnell's lawyer, I have no choice but to file an injunction against Treecorp for violating its eminent domain charter."

Gage spluttered. "You can't do that! Tyree and everything on it belongs to Treecorp!"

Strickland snorted. "Read your charter, Mr. Gage. I have requested a full investigation by Federation Corporate Compliance. I recommend you inform your superiors. Good day." The holo disappeared.

Liam couldn't help but grin as impotent rage filled Gage's face. He knew the feeling well. The assessor spun, waved his goons back to their land speeders, and left.

Liam's breath whooshed out. His heart felt light for the first time in months. He slapped Marken on the shoulder. "Thank you, son."

Clara bolted off the porch and tackled Liam's legs. "Did it work, Grandpa?"

"It did, Sweetie. The land is ours. The next few years are gonna be lean, though. We're gonna have to grow something new. Soybeans maybe."

"You've started something big, you know," Marken said, gesturing toward the smoky horizon from a hundred burning orchards. "Things are hard now, but I see a bright future for Tyree. I heard some of the neighbors talking about making you the new governor."

"But I'm no politician!"

"That's what makes you perfect for the job. You can build something new, something better from the broken pieces of Tyree. You up for it?"

Liam picked up Clara, held her tight, but didn't answer. He had kept what he valued most. His family. His home.

He'd take the future as it came.

About the Author

David Hankins writes from the thriving cornfields of Iowa. His writing journey began years ago in Germany as he made up stories to convince his daughter to go to sleep, which always backfired. Those midnight ramblings developed into a passion for creating new worlds while exploring the idiosyncrasies of this one.

David joined the US Army after college and, through some glitch in the bureaucracy, convinced them to fund his wanderlust for twenty years. He has lived in and traveled through much of Europe, central Asia, and the United States. Eventually, he hopes to fund his wanderlust through writing.

*****~~~~~*****

Amphibios

by Julie Biegner

The two girls had just one thing in common: a burning distaste for the times. It stemmed from vastly different logics, but it was enough.

Asia was what they call an amphibiphile. Lover of all-things-amphibian, driven all the more frenzied by the creature's extinction. It had started when she was two years old and her mother handed her a stuffed animal, Fred, bulging eyes popping out of its silly-shaped frog body. Asia would suck on those eyeballs like synthetic-flavored lollipops, and VR-boosted recreations from her childhood showed streams of her sitting there, sucking on those big frog eyes, her mom behind her, doubled over in between bouts of coughing and laughter. Her mom was gone now, but Fred was still there.

Cazzy was what they call a raging bitch. She blamed the entire Last Generation, known as Gen Z, for excavating the earth to the digital carcass it now was. This happened to include her mother, who disappeared before Cazzy could hold onto a memory of her, and her father, a mid-level engineer whose eSports gambling addiction had taken off not long after.

So here's what you need to know before you can understand why they did it: Before they ever met, they each yearned for that which they could never have.

At least not through those warped simulations that made up the Stream, those virtual recreations that piecemealed the world into a functional metaverse, stitching together web hits, social media feeds, and surveillance footage and feeding it back to the masses in 360-degrees of simulated reality.

Perhaps it was life before the Stream they desired, back before the Sixth Extinction climaxed with God's Wrath, when supply chains crumbled and disasters struck like a plague taking out the sick, the poor, the elderly, the children, the homeless, the lonely, the forgotten.

For a moment, it had been tough goings in America. Yet resilience abounds for the strong-willed, and those that ultimately survived did so gallantly: they flew in strawberries from far away lands; stored slabs of beef in their newly built walk-in freezers; amassed that two-ply Charmin; packed their pantries; locked their doors; securitized their homes; and when the worst was over, emerged plump.

Just as the weakest of the humans met their Darwinian fate, so too did the fauna and the flora. It wasn't long before the most magnificent of prehistoric beasts died out nearly overnight, when the last frog was overtaken by a poisonous fungi spreading hungrily through the tropics.

This was God's Wrath. This was the past two adolescent girls longed for.

Asia and Cazzy had no one to point them in wiser directions. Like all lost souls before them, they were dreamers.

It is dreamers, after all, who hold the power to change the course of history.

. . .

"This is bullshit."

92

Amphibios

The message popped into thin air, appearing with a *ding* over the clouds Asia was watching lazily beyond the treetops.

"*Bullshit,*" the word reappeared, vibrating in emotion.

Asia nodded, sending a grunt of agreement in response.

Cazzy's follow up came instantly: "I just *can't believe* they're shutting down Bankurt High."

Asia dismissed the notification, mesmerized by her surroundings: the howl of the wind; the rustling of the grass; the clouds above her changing form both slowly and all at once.

Another *whoosh* arrived just as a duck-like cloud waddled its way toward the sun.

"Dude, it's ridiculous. These corporate dicks take over the school, spouting their *bullshit* about innovation with"—and animated air quotes flew up into the clouds here—"*proven* technological measures to temper socio-behavioral issues of our generation through *data-driven simulated* learning curricula. And now they're shutting Bankurt down. What a joke."

Cazzy's voice landed rushed and shrill in Asia's ear, as though her best friend were lying next to her on the grass rather than miles away in her room. A series of *pings* quickly followed, and three news articles popped up, hovering transparently over the weeds in Asia's lower line of vision:

Agram CEO J. Daily, Jr. announces new initiative to boost kids' techno-social skills.

Agram donating high-speed Stream access to eligible low-income Bankurt households.

New D-3 drone delivery center replacing Bankurt Lab in boon to local economy.

Asia sighed. The two girls had been pinging messages back and forth since the school had sent the news an hour ago: Bankurt High was closing, the school's Lab—its only physical manifestation—was being shuttered, and students would be siphoned off to virtual hubs across the country according to their most recent test scores.

She watched as the duck-shaped cloud transformed into whisps before disappearing entirely. Another *whoosh* arrived.

"Asia, my weird-ass, Kermit-loving, bug-eyed beauty: It's time to fuck shit up. We're about to be separated. Once the Lab is closed, our plan is shot to hell."

The final cloud in Asia's sky disappeared, and the grass field she was lying in slowly morphed into a shabby carpet. The girl now sat in a small, dimly lit room. Her 15-minute trial of a simulated grass meadow was up.

Asia removed her headset, rubbed her eyes in exhaustion and finally sent off a voice note of her own.

"I know. Remember what I told you when we first met?"

. . .

The Lab had been a community donation from Agram, announced amid rumors that a parents' group was pushing in-person learning. The Bankurt High School Lab became a central hub, 3,000 individual stalls for students to hook into their Stream classes with high-speed access to 1,000+ simulation worlds—expensive sim-worlds that most Bankurt families could not afford.

Cazzy hated the flashy titanium Lab headsets, opting to use her own outdated model made of clunky plastics. She despised the "hall monitors," AI bots that roamed the Lab's corridors to ticket students found outside their booths during class. The only part she didn't mind was the ride to and from the Lab, taking the fortified self-driving zoom-boards through the wretched streets and ungodly heat. She would stare out the window, watching the desecrated landscape outside with curious envy.

Amphibios

On that fateful day, Cazzy was meant to be preparing a history report about how the global food supply had been resurrected with nutrients scraped from the ocean floors. But rather than being deep in a simulation of salt water sludge, she was encrypted-messaging in a group chat of the Visceral Resistancers.

The Visceral Resistancers were a group of teenagers who relied on performative actions to express their dissatisfaction with the digital world order: an interface disruption here, digital vandalism there, occasional anonymous threats of leaked secrets. It didn't amount to much, but Cazzy found it an amusing way to pass the time.

Just as she double-tapped her approval on a post from VReedomRider69, Cazzy's surroundings distorted, and the simulation around her blurred before settling on an empty black void. *Damn headset*, Cazzy thought, before glumly taking it off and kicking open the accordion doors to try another booth.

But rather than opening smoothly, the doors clattered into a frail human form that crumbled to the ground in an instant.

Cazzy swore. "You okay?" she asked hesitantly, as the body on the ground began to stir.

"I think so," came the reply, breezy but even-toned.

The girl on the ground contorted herself into a cross-legged position but stayed put, effectively blocking Cazzy from leaving her booth.

"Well, good," Cazzy said. "But in that case I need to find a new booth, so if you could—"

The girl cut her off, peering up at her from the floor with a blank look. "You're Cazzy, right? I think we had Sim-Phys-Ed together. I loved that class."

Cazzy had a flash of their tenth year, a virtual bowling class consisting of countless digital faces she could not now remember.

"Yeah, I'm sure you bowled great fake-strikes. I'll be sure to tell my pops, he'll be glad to hear he did something right at Agram. Listen, a hall bot is bound to turn up any minute, so we should. . . "

She trailed off as the girl quickly raised an eyebrow on her otherwise stoic face.

"Don't worry about that. You mean your dad works for Agram?"

Cazzy's temper flared at the girl's aloofness. "Maybe you don't need to worry, but I already have two citations this month, and I can't afford another fine."

"Is he a sim-creator? Systems engineer? Drone-technician?" The girl spoke unhurriedly but with a newfound curiosity.

"Dude, he's a sell-out sim creator shilling for Agram, but who gives a crap. Look, we really gotta—"

"I programmed this hall's bot, it won't come for another 20 minutes. What security clearance does he have, do you know?"

Cazzy was speechless for a moment, a rarity, looking at the girl across from her. She was still pretzel-legged on the floor, cherry-colored crumpled hair framing her oversized olive glasses, a perpetually blank look but for her head tilted, awaiting a response.

Slowly, a smile crept onto Cazzy's face as she plopped down next to the girl in the middle of the hallway, leaned back against the booth, and fell into full-bellied laughter.

. . .

That had been over a year ago.

"Yes, I remember," Cazzy said now. "You said you had a plan, and when the time came, you'd be ready." She spoke slowly, not accusatory, not with Asia.

"It's time. I'm ready. Here's how it will go."

. . .

Asia twiddled her thumbs restlessly, as she waited for Cazzy's response to the final details of what the girls

96

had deemed The Plan. It was quiet in the apartment she shared with her Aunt Nel, who snored lightly across the room.

Cazzy's reply dinged its arrival:

"It's perfect. Foolproof."

A second text followed: "Okay, it's ridiculous. But it will work. We are about to Fuck Some Shit Up," Cazzy cooed, clearly daydreaming about the kudos she'd receive from the VR.

Asia's stomach lurched. "The point isn't to fuck anything up. We need to stay focused," she replied.

"I know you find this hard to believe, Asia, but some things are worse than failure. Like not taking this opportunity while we have it. Or dying a virgin."

"This is serious. We're committing a criminal offense, and it's not like Agram is known for its leniency. Some of the stories about the ePolice on these chat boards are wild."

Cazzy read Asia's message over a few times. She was alone in her room, looking out the single window in the desolate one bedroom she occupied with her father. Outside, Cazzy could see drones flying in an asynchronous dance through what she knew was an oppressive, all-consuming heat.

"Asia, we've talked about the risks. To use lawyer-talk: 'Under Public-Private Resolution 1504, all Stream users are subject to Agram's jurisprudence. Unauthorized Stream access is a felony open to prosecution by Agram's private criminal procedures.' If they trace this to us, we are fucked."

"The most likely outcome is that we'd end up in one of their simulated prison cells for up to a decade."

Cazzy nodded to herself, still looking out the window as she pinged back: "So, Saturday?"

Asia, for all her sense and rationality, couldn't help it. She smiled. "Saturday."

. . .

Asia loved frogs, because they were bold. Fearless despite their delicate bodies, resilient despite their skin so thin, so flimsy. And yet there they were, bellowing through the night, an unending screaming cacophony. Primordial and unignorable.

She loved them too because they could blend—naked to the eye while everpresent. Ancient, prehistoric, had survived the apocalypses of the 12th, 15th, 19th centuries—survivors because they could blend. Until they couldn't anymore.

The Goliath Bullfrog was the crème de la crème.

Asia had first discovered it in an advertisement on the Stream, when she heard a deep voice booming:

A journey awaits. Rappel down a waterfall. Glide through the long-lost Amazon. Connect with ancient wildlife. This is your chance to Journey Through the Tropics.

And there—for three seconds, balanced elegantly on a rock before leaping gracefully behind a tree limb—was the Goliath Bullfrog.

The *Tropics* simulation was, of course, more than a month's rent for most Bankurt families. But Asia became obsessed, scouring the darkweb for its taxonomy, behavior, traits. She restored a salvaged Wikipedia entry detailing the beast's toes fully webbed, its dorsal coloration a green sienna, the abdomen a yellow-orange. The words clung to her, stoking a fire in her belly that drove her onward.

Her content search was in vain. Agram's ePolice division, notoriously militant, applied steep paywalls on luxury sim content. On the chat boards she frequented, Asia heard occasional rumblings of darker deeds: digital disappearances and identity wipes, rumors that the ePolice's militancy might extend beyond their digital borders; but she preferred not to engage with conspiracies.

Cazzy, for her part, loved to theorize about Agram's wicked ways. Which is why when Asia raised the idea of stealing her dad's work credentials, she was in before even hearing the rest of The Plan.

The Plan: simple, impossible, inevitable.

The Plan was to hack onto the Stream's servers from the Lab, enter the *Tropics* simulation, find the Goliath Bullfrog, and take a sample of its digital genome. Asia would then replicate it, change minor digital-DNA sequencing to become untraceable and load it onto her personal Stream.

Meanwhile, Cazzy could pull off a truly one-of-a-kind stunt for the VR, letting the digital footprint of the eFrog loose on the Stream and sending millions of frog faces in a cyber-attack on unsuspecting users: a bored businessman trying on different skins; a spoiled teenager dancing in a music video with pop star Grady Owens; a married woman eBoning a colleague in a private, life-like jacuzzi.

And then, ripping them out of their sensation of reality, the grotesque amphibian face would appear and let loose its strident call.

It would be the most visible move of the VR yet.

. . .

Here is what you have got to understand. Past records make it clear: Daily, Jr. never actually cared for the Stream.

Consider **Voice Note #1550,** captured March 15, 2072, days after Daily, Sr.'s passing:

It finally happened. True to his word, the old man left me with nothing, straight empty-handed but for domain over the business and a narcissist's belief that he had saved the world.

I can't blame him, really. Pops birthed Agram out of his very own cognitive womb, nurturing the little runt through the tumultuous end of the world. He created a giant, an inflection point on humanity's existential

*timeline. So I, his only son, have but one purpose on this
wretched planet: continue the legacy.*

Cheers to that. See you in the next life, old man.

Whether he wanted it or not, Agram flourished
with Daily, Jr. at the helm. But the obligation of the
legacy weighed on him. He developed what some say was
a paranoid, inflated sense of self. Others describe it as a
savvy business sense.

Either way, by the time The Plan was ready for
action, Agram had supplanted the state in everything but
name, yet Daily, Jr's sense of foreboding had only grown.

. . .

The girls were shivering, squeezed together there
in a Lab stall, not knowing whether it was the chill of the
A/C blowing lightly on them or the anticipation that had
the hairs on their arms alert.

Cazzy was already hooked in, using mark-up tools
to write *'V.R.'* in big looping letters as a tattoo on her
pixel-perfect wrist.

Asia paused a moment, her eyes caught on a spot
of green peeking out of her bag: Fred's worn webbed toes.

She tried to remember that day, a lifetime ago, her
mother's auburn hair, crumpled like hers, brown eyes
crinkling in warmth as she handed over the stuffed toy
frog. But she couldn't remember a thing, could only see
the recreation of that day replaying in her head, the Stream
clip she had savored, watched over and over before
Agram had removed data storage from its basic user
privileges and the memory had disappeared with it.

She sighed, rubbed her eyes and secured the lab's
shiny AG-marked headset to her head, where it sat
glistening like a crown.

Underneath her own bulky plastic headset, Cazzy
smiled.

Asia then used one hand to hold her best friend's
sweating palm in hers, and the other to hit 'Enter'.

. . .

Looking back on it all, perhaps you are left wondering: How do two girls from Bankurt take down a tech conglomerate that had emerged as a fascist state?

Well, they don't.

Agram's ePolice tracked the girls down 90 seconds after Asia hit Enter. Three minutes later, unbranded drones surrounded the school. They lit it up.

In the days to come, the Stream's media tickers briefly mentioned two hackers had died after, tragically but illegally, trespassing on the site of a planned demolition of Agram's private property.

What two girls from Bankurt did, though, was spark a match.

Because when the Visceral Resistancers, who Cazzy had been livestreaming with from the Lab, found themselves in possession of live footage of a drone attack on Bankurt High with two teen girls inside, they released it nearly in real time. It led to the highest VR recruitment numbers in the group's history.

It was 23 years later that a faction of the VR broke off into a militarized political arm, one that, 12 years after that, hacked a DR9 delivery drone to drop a single grenade on Agram HQ. It was a hack that set in motion a conflict that culminated in the year 2147, when the Stream broke wide open, eMarkets collapsed, and the second earth-shattering depression in a century took place.

And the society that emerged in its stead? It's not perfect—we're not perfect. But we tell the stories of the past; even two girls who had no reason to meet, yet who hand in sweaty hand lit a match. It was the kind of fire that Asia felt churning in her gut, that drove her on an absurd mission to find a rendering of a frog, the kind she took for motivation.

But it wasn't motivation.

It was rage.

###

About the Author

Julie Biegner is an emerging writer originally from Los Angeles, California. Now based in Asheville, North Carolina, she loves short stories of cli-fi and speculative fiction and enjoys deep-diving into the stories of her Asheville writing group.

*****~~~~~*****

Earth's Last Immortals

by Erin Cullen

Kiley didn't even have the decency to let me know that she was planning to die.

It could have been an accident, I suppose. She'd been hiking alone, at night, a risky prospect even for someone as practiced at survival as the two of us. Her body was found at the bottom of a cliff, and foul play was quickly eliminated as a possibility. She hardly knew anyone in this century, certainly hadn't had any enemies. She'd left her small hiking pack at the top, probably trusting her body to remain intact long enough that she could be identified from the ID chip embedded in her wrist. There had been no dirt under her fingernails, no signs of struggle at all on her body, which I'd been called to the city morgue to identify. There had been no flecks of blood at the edge of the cliff, no scrapes in the dirt evidencing a slip at the top of the mountain. I'd checked the top of the cliff myself, positioned my own feet at the absolute edge, even wobbled on purpose to figure out if an accidental fall was possible. I survived.

. . .

At the beginning, the founders had always liked to point out that, despite fears of overpopulation, the burgeoning immortality and climate restoration movements had similar premises: we have work to do today if we want to survive tomorrow.

There was the philosophical element, of course—people who planned to be around to see the distant future had reason to ensure that the world wouldn't become a ruin. But the stronger parallel was the biological argument—how the possibility of human immortality that had developed through the history written in our cells, matched the interventions that we needed to create to save the world.

The keys were discovered in the early twenty-first century, and brought to market not long after. Many, early on, called the movement crazy—what kind of life could one live with daily handfuls of pills instead of food, a moratorium against exposure to direct sunlight, a brutal and exhaustive exercise regimen? A long one, someone once said. And in a certain light, none of it was new. There were echoes of the same elements in ancient myths and religious traditions, most notably, for 21st-century social media commentators, vampires.

The regimen works through the same cellular machinery that developed to keep life going since its very beginning. But those cellular systems are lazy. They only activate when cells are under duress. And the most effective duress is that imposed by nutrient deficiency; the original duress that inspired our single-celled ancestors to develop these systems in the first place. The regimen ensures that we won't die, at least not of old age. But to partner with those parts of ourselves, we have to limit how we live.

So many had asked: how dare we focus on immortality when the planet is in crisis? But the key to immortality turned out to also be the key to human flourishing beyond the excesses of the twentieth century: restraint.

After five hundred years, I'm finally willing to admit that it was probably easier for me than it would have been for other people. The first few weeks of the regimen were so brutal that I couldn't have imagined, back then, that it might be even worse for other people. But other people had jobs lifting heavy things, or children to mind in their off-hours, ailments that the regimen exacerbated to intolerable levels, and stressful lives that necessitated a bit of pleasure. I'd had a well-paid job writing software to replace administrative assistants and lawyers and a manager who didn't care if I spent an entire morning staring despondently out the window, waiting for the brain fog that came with the hunger to lift. For a home I'd had an apartment two blocks from the office in an immaculate building with a gym on the first floor. I'd had no responsibilities to keep me from sleeping twelve hours a night as the compounds I was consuming instead of food broke into my cells and repaired the day's ruptures in my DNA, reversing the aging process that humanity had once believed to be inevitable.

I'd pushed through the grueling first few weeks because I knew that I had nothing of substance to gain by giving up. I was forty-eight years old, unmarried and childless, with no family except for a deadbeat younger brother who only ever called to ask for money. If I had kept living my life as I had been, as nearly everyone else had, back then, all that lay ahead of me was another forty or so bleak years of the same mind-numbing work that I knew was only leading to an even more unjust society than we already had, the same calls from my brother, and occasional boring nights out with my mostly younger coworkers. My twenties and thirties had been sucked up by school and then my father's long battle with cancer, followed by my mother's with dementia. Dating had been my main preoccupation for a while after that, and yet I had nothing to show for it. Women who would have me were established in their own careers, often with teenage children, and couldn't give me the new life I was seeking. I didn't want to try to fumble my way into someone else's family—I wanted to build one of my own, that I could call my own, after I'd sacrificed so many years for the family I'd originally been stuck with.

At first, I thought that I would only follow the regimen for six months or so—decrease my biological age by ten or fifteen years, find a woman to marry and have children with, and grow old with her. And I'd tried, for a bit, but after starting the regimen I found that everyone I met shied away from me, either intimidated or disgusted by my lifestyle. Everyone but the other immortals, of course. In Internet chatrooms and occasional in-person meetups, I found a community of driven, ambitious people who made me feel like I was growing into a better, more exciting person just by being around them. When six months had passed and my biological age hit its anticipated low of thirty-one, I didn't stop. I had found the family I'd been looking for.

I quit my job and joined a speaking circuit touting the regimen, an uphill battle that we'd optimistically predicted, at the time, might last a few dozen years. After all, we had the data showing that most people didn't want to die. There were people who had started with too high a chronological age to be helped much by the regimen giving impassioned speeches about how heartbroken they were about everything they would miss due to the random luck of being born twenty or forty years too early. My niche was a triumphant story of the lost decades of my young adulthood, and how I felt like the regimen had given me those years of my life back, how the regimen had allowed me to not have to make the hard choice between caring for my parents and building my own life after they passed. Despite the strength of our messaging, people only trickled in. Everyone else was unwilling to give up food and alcohol and drugs and sunlight, preferring to maintain their lifestyles until they died pointlessly in the frail, diseased bodies they'd sculpted. Or so we'd complained to each other at the time.

After a while, I'd jumped off the speaking circuit to be with a woman I loved, who, like me, wanted to raise a family. By then we were both making enough interest off our investments to live lives of leisure, and we were happy for those years. We'd had only one child, Gianna, because Eleanor, my then-partner, hadn't wanted to go off the regimen for a second pregnancy. I'd doted on Gianna and taught her everything I knew, and she had as happy a childhood as anyone ever had, even amidst the economic and climate crises that defined the late twenty-first century. I'd been even more pleased that Eleanor and I had remained independent and in no need of her help, and she'd gone on to have a wonderful career developing clean energy technologies. The only serious arguments we ever had were about the regimen. Gianna had never wanted to start it, and the fights grew more and more bitter as she turned forty, and fifty, and sixty. Eleanor and I were still in our thirties biologically, and our relationship was turning cold and rocky, long run its course but for our shared love for Gianna, and our shared belief that we didn't dare split up until she stopped being so *childish* and started the regimen. When she turned seventy, we gave up. Gianna died at eighty-nine.

It was only a few years later that immortality finally began to appeal to the masses. Not long after Gianna passed came a golden age of hope and individualism, the first generation of youths in more than a century brought up in prosperity and possibility, with the option to sculpt their lives to a purpose beyond averting disaster. Society had been overhauled during Gianna's life, and the youth of the latest generation could take hope for granted in a way that no one had since my childhood, before the climate crisis had started to destroy glaciers, then islands, then cities. Art and travel boomed. Initiatives in space exploration made life seem unlimited.

Earlier generations just above these youths that felt like they had missed out. They had emerged into adulthood twenty or thirty years previous, before the climate crisis started to fade from the public consciousness and the self-sacrificing, collectivist principles that had heralded its end were replaced with individual goals and dreams. With all the death that the climate crisis had wrought, fears about overpopulation (which some had always believed were just excuses to avoid the difficulties of the regimen) were extinguished. The immortal community swelled, going from a niche curiosity to a mainstream movement in a few years. My chronological age was over 150, and suddenly the several thousand immortals remaining from the twentieth century were a precious resource, treated as precognitive wells of wisdom.

An early addition to the community in those days was Trina, who I quickly bonded with over shared experiences of feeling like we'd missed out on our young adulthoods. She'd realized in her forties that she was transgender, and wanted to re-experience youth in a body that could fully feel like hers.

But then, in youth, she wanted to celebrate it. She wanted to go out drinking and dancing and dining and not be beholden to twice-daily handfuls of pills. She wanted to be young in a way that I, too, never had, and for ten years, she and I had gone off the regimen. Those years passed in a blur of endorphins and joy and wild, mortal love, and I forgot about age entirely until I started to wake up sore from nights out dancing, pull muscles in my back doing simple chores, feel old injuries throb in damp weather. The appeal of the regimen, once again, outweighed the costs.

Trina kissed me in a bittersweet mutual goodbye, and I returned to an immortal community where I was heralded as a respected elder. I began to tell my story again, and eventually got bored of speaking and wrote a book instead. The young immortals were overwhelming, and I found even more comfort than before in reconnecting in the few from my generation that remained. The ranks were already thinning. Some had died from illness or accidents, and a few had made the same choice as Trina and had exited the community to live out the rest of their lives like their ancestors had been forced to. Some joined space exploration missions, crewing ships that might never return to Earth, an opportunity available only to people who had reached a chronological age exceeding 100.

I continued to write, first more memoirs, then history, for generations of people who couldn't fathom the political turmoil and primitive technology of my early life. Immortality wavered in popularity, and finally waned, first among people who remained on Earth. A movement had been sweeping through to resuscitate the diverse cultures that had melded together in recent decades, and that work and appreciation for Earth's natural environment became Earth's trademark in the developing interplanetary human community. Immortality, despite its long history, was too modern for this new zeitgeist. People wanted to live as their ancestors had, because it was the way their ancestors had lived. Some used the regimen on the Mars and Alpha Centauri settlements, but life there was hard, and immortality was impractical for a civilization running on limited life support. Outside of the deep space missions, the regimen fell out of favor.

By the early twenty-sixth century, the immortal community in the city I'd been living in seemed to all but vanish. Gatherings that had once swamped ballrooms soon barely filled houses, then people trickled away until only ten, then five, were left, and then it was only Kiley and me.

. . .

The argument that I thought was silliest, early on, was, *won't you be lonely?*

As the founders had retorted, everyone around you could be immortal too. Who could even know who would eventually outlive who? But that had been meaningless to me. I'd been lonely already, in my previous life. If loneliness was a good enough reason to give up on living, then I may as well not have lived at all.

After Kiley died, I understood better what those critics had meant. From a certain perspective, life is endless—there will always be more books than a single individual could ever read, more art than one could ever view, more meaning to make of art you've seen before, more people to meet and grow apart from and meet again, more skills to learn, more places to travel, and places you've before been made new again.

But life doesn't come for free. We have to choose between the asceticism of the regimen and the consequences of forgoing it, between the difficulty of work and the discomfort of existing without contributing, between the messy negotiations of relationships and the ache of loneliness. Every second, for immortals, represents a choice between life and death.

Nature gave us an easy, graceful way out. A life broken into certain, predictable stages, perhaps a legacy, boundaries around what to do and where to go next, a body that eventually decayed and settled back into the component parts from which it came. There was a dignity to death that I hadn't appreciated early on, beyond the peace that I suppose must come with believing in reincarnation or an afterlife. There is power in an ending, in truly believing that without you, the world will go on. Believing that takes strength, when there's another option. For the founders, and millennia of alchemists and scholars before them, the slow surety of aging hadn't held up against the allure of life.

And for Kiley, that allure had faded.

I wonder how long she had been planning it. Jumping off a cliff instead of going through the process of

Dignified Death at a clinic is unnecessary for someone as old as her. She would have had a short waiting period and no other prerequisites had she simply submitted an application. She could have spent her last week of life celebrating, imbibing every hedonic experience humanity has ever dreamed into existence, or lived even longer like that, and not submitted an application until her hair greyed and her joints began to ache, or even waited until she died naturally of frailty and disease. But she had jumped, still feeling the slight discomfort of cold and hunger that never quite go away, in a body that could have lived on indefinitely. Maybe in that single second the pain of life was too much and the rewards too few, and the cliff was right there.

With Kiley gone, I was more alone than I'd been since before I started the regimen. If I was standing near a cliff when I heard of her death, I might have taken one step closer.

. . .

I considered going off the regimen again and living out my days in dreary routine, like I'd thought would be my fate five hundred years before, but I signed up for a deep-space mission instead. "Finally got bored of this rock?" a startlingly familiar voice called from behind me on the first day of training.

I turned around and all but fell into Trina's arms. "You're still alive!" She'd let herself age a little further than I ever had, and her hair was streaked with gray, her body heavier, her face more lined. But she was alive, and I was alive, and we still had unimaginable adventures ahead of us.

"I wasn't finished with that kind of life when you were," she said. "But it turned out I wasn't finished with this one either."

We won't actually live forever, of course. One day the universe will expand so far that stars and their planets will splinter and disappear, and the likelihood that any

111

human lives long enough to perish in the heat death of the universe is infinitesimal. Perhaps one day I will even give up. But for now, life is endless, and I want to live.

About the Author

Erin Cullen studied neuroscience and English at University of Pittsburgh and is currently a graduate student in neuroscience at University of Vermont. She spends her time outside the lab hiking Vermont's beautiful mountains and dreaming up stories about science and the future.

*****~~~~*****

Last Light in the Dark

by Shannon Fox

"I can't do this," Mikhail Radnovsky said.

He dropped the script he was reading onto his agent's desk and looked up. Annie was smiling that too-wide smile, one that was all teeth and gums. A smile he knew well after ten years of working together.

Through the window behind her, the lights scattered throughout the city shone like beacons in the semi-darkness. When humanity abandoned Old Earth centuries ago, they'd selected the planet, Telkeon, as the cradle for their new civilization. Their empire had grown until it encompassed dozens of worlds like this one, behemoths of metal and glass and light.

"So they rewrote your character. It's easy money, Radnovsky. You like easy money, don't you?" Annie asked.

His eyes jumped back to her. "When I signed with you, I told you there were three things I wouldn't do in any comm program. Nude scenes, kid stuff, and genocide."

"It's not genocide."

"It's genocide with aliens."

She spread her hands, as if to say, *does it matter?*

"It matters to me," he said. "This isn't the role I agreed to."

As an awkward silence descended, everything in the office felt much too close. It was a small space, made smaller by the number of trinkets and memorabilia Annie insisted on displaying. The space dripped personality, but it also seemed to suggest that the personality and the mind it belonged to had lost its balance, tipping inexorably toward the weird.

"Does that mean you're passing?" Annie asked.

His heart said yes, but his head said no. He wanted to tell stories that moved people, that mattered, and this wasn't it. However, he had his sister, Irina, and her son, Kolya, to worry about. The boy had a rare blood disorder that required regular transfusions that Irina couldn't afford with just her salary alone.

Radnovsky scrubbed a hand across his face and then ran his fingers through his golden hair. It was a bit longer than he liked, but Annie said the style suited him. Made it easier for her to sell him to casting directors, too.

"I've worked with Babbitt before," Radnovsky said. "Perhaps he'd be open to making some changes."

. . .

"Absolutely not."

Spittle flew from Gregory Babbitt's lips, and his cheeks turned an alarming shade of red-purple. Then, as if reconsidering his outburst, the director leaned back in his padded desk chair and rolled his shoulders before continuing in a calmer tone.

"That is the story, Radnovsky. It's what the audience wants. And we're all here to make money. Even you, or you wouldn't be here thinking you can change my mind."

Babbitt rested his meaty hands flat on the desk in front of him. It was a leviathan of matte black steel. Meant to intimidate just as much as the man who sat behind it. "You're too idealistic for this business. I thought that when we worked together before, but back then, I needed someone who could embody optimism. That rah-rah glorious future bullshit."

Radnovsky rubbed his hands against his pants, as he considered what to say. The fabric was thin from too many washings.

Babbitt wasn't the first to suggest he might not be cut out for this line of work, though Radnovsky loved it. Loved acting and loved storytelling. Most of all, he loved carrying on the family legacy. Especially now that he, Irina, and Kolya were all that was left of the once great Radnovsky family of entertainers, whose roots stretched all the way back to Old Earth. If he wasn't an actor, he didn't know who he would be.

"Look," Babbitt said. "If you don't want the role, I'll find somebody else. There are twenty other guys with pretty blue eyes just like you that would love the part."

"No." Radnovsky saw Kolya's face, the nine-year-old's gap-toothed smile. "I want it. I understand what my job is. Just act. Don't ask questions."

"Good," the director said. He motioned toward the door. "I have a few calls to make before people show up and bother me. Make sure you're back on set in two hours. I run a tight ship, as I'm sure you remember."

Summarily dismissed, Radnovsky stood up and exited the office.

On the soundstage outside, the set crew was still working. He imagined they'd been up most of the last few days. Nobody shot on location anymore. Not with the need to turn a completed product quickly.

Digital displays covered the wall outside Babbitt's office, each one showcasing a different comm program. Radnovsky walked a few feet until he found the one they'd done together. *Moonlight in the Abyss*. The story of the first colonists who journeyed from Old Earth to their new

115

home in the Cordat Medalia system. It was a first-rate drama, filled with meditations about the true nature of courage, finding resilience in dark times, and holding onto hope against insurmountable odds.

Exactly the sort of comm program that didn't get made anymore.

As he watched the credits scroll by on the display, he heard his grandfather's words. It'd been over a decade since Radnovsky had lost him, but he still heard the soft, strong voice as if he were standing next to him.

"Artists teach people about their humanity, Mikhail."

Radnovsky sighed. When grandfather was his age, art still had a soul. Now, it was just another commodity. Instead of inspiration and ideas and grand messages about what it means to be human, all that was required was a puppet to smile and say the lines.

The gold rush of planetary expansion, when the Cordat Medalia first settled this system and its half a dozen habitable planets, meant that it now required a massive amount of human capital to sustain what they'd built. There was plenty of work, though much of it was unskilled and low paying. Monitoring a screen all day. Making sure this or that machine didn't error out. Billions of people had the type of job where they staved off the monotony by watching or listening to endless hours of comm programming. All they wanted was to fill their minds with emptiness. And Radnovsky and other artists like him provided.

It wasn't that he couldn't switch careers. He could. Acting paid better than most things though, even if it wasn't anything close to what actors used to make on Old Earth. And he needed the money.

He looked back at the soundstage where the crew was in constant motion, building out the alien city of Laporsky.

For Kolya and Irina, he would do this. He would make it work.

. . .

For three weeks, he managed it. He showed up, did what he was told, and didn't complain. It was far from his best work, but then, his best work wasn't required anymore.

At the start of the fourth week, Annie got him on one of those late-night interview shows. It would be one of the first press junkets for the new comm program. Radnovsky wasn't looking forward to it, but this too was the work. To smile and say nice things about Babbitt and his co-stars. To build excitement for the new program. He knew his job, and he would do it, however grudgingly.

The show was held on a small soundstage in front of a live audience of only two dozen people. An array of cameras would broadcast the interview live from Telkeon throughout the system. Radnovsky and the host, Poppy, sat across from each other in identical plush armchairs. The curved wall behind them was made up of dozens of digital displays, each showing something different. A scent of lemons hung in the air, the artificial fragrance pumped through the vents.

Poppy was young, with pale pink hair and eyes a peculiar shade of blue-gray. She'd had so many body modifications she looked more like someone's warped idea of a beautiful woman, rather than someone who was actually beautiful.

For the first half hour of the interview, Poppy volleyed question after question at Radnosky who gamely hit every one back over the net. None of her questions were hard, and he knew exactly what to say. He thought of Annie and Babbitt, watching the interview from the silver room backstage. They must both be breathing a sigh of relief that things were going so well.

Poppy looked down at the notes in her lap, and then back up. She licked her upper lip as she considered what to say next. And in that moment, he knew he was in trouble.

"Your new program has already met with its share of criticism," she said. "Some people think it glorifies genocide, which your director has categorically denied. Others, while acknowledging the content issue, find it palatable because the comm program describes the genocide of an alien race, rather than humans. I'm wondering what your take is."

Radnovsky swallowed and reached for the glass of water on the table in front of him. He knew what he *should* say, which was to be intentionally vague and deny everything. Yet, what he wanted to say was something quite different.

After taking a long drink of water, he replaced the glass. Then, he looked back toward the row of cameras and the live studio audience beyond them. His eyes fell on a young man who reminded him of Kolya—of who the boy might be one day.

"Would you like me to repeat the question?" Poppy asked.

He turned to her and stared deeply into her odd-colored eyes.

"No," he said. "I heard you."

A pause.

Then, the words tumbled out before he could take them back. "I think the comm program does present a romanticized view of genocide. And that's wrong in all contexts. When our ancestors left Old Earth to settle the stars, we didn't find anything else living out here. But that doesn't mean we never will. If we find ourselves faced with a similar moral quandary one day, it will be on us to make the right choice."

Poppy opened her mouth to comment, but Radnovsky barreled on. He couldn't leave his thoughts half-finished.

"That's what art does for us. It holds up a mirror so we can see ourselves accurately, the good and the ugly. We should be wary of anything that tells us otherwise."

His face burned as he waited for the host to say something, every beat of silence more uncomfortable than the last. He wondered how Babbitt and Annie had received his remarks. Probably not well.

Across from him, Poppy frowned, her brow wrinkling. She seemed to be listening to something he couldn't hear. Perhaps she had an ear modification, allowing her to receive messages from backstage.

"We're going to take a short break," she said, plastering on a smile as she looked at the cameras and the studio audience. "When we come back, we'll be talking about what else you can expect when this comm program hits the streams later this month."

Radnovsky found Babbitt and Annie back in the silver room.

"That was absolute bullshit," Babbitt spat, when Radnovsky walked in. The director looked as if there were at least a dozen other things he wanted to say and none of them nice. The only reason he seemed to be holding back was because Annie was there.

"I'm sorry," Radnovsky said, though it was only half true. Mostly, he was sorry he'd let things go this far.

"Don't even bother going back out there," said Babbitt. "You're done. Now get out of my sight."

Radnovsky looked from the director to his agent. There was no trace of a smile on Annie's face as she met his gaze.

"You should have just said no."

"Probably."

He took off the microphone the tech crew had given him and handed it to Annie, Then, unsure what to say or do next, he shoved his hands in his pockets and left.

. . .

Radnovsky woke to the darkness of early morning. Staring up at the living room ceiling, he enjoyed a moment's peace, until the events of the night before came flooding back.

He tasted bile, as his stomach soured. Throwing off the blanket, he got up and stumbled to the hall bathroom, pausing only to shut the door behind him. He didn't want to wake his sister and Kolya.

He dry-heaved, but nothing came up. Then he rinsed his mouth out with cold water from the sink and splashed some onto his face. It felt good, as if he were washing away the grime of who he'd been these last few weeks.

Yet the anxiety sat in his gut like a lead ball. He walked over to Kolya's room and eased the door open. The boy was curled up in his blankets, his hair mussed from sleep. His chest rose and fell rhythmically.

Closing the door again, Radnovsky went back to the living room and paced, turning over his options. By the time the first light of starrise crept through the living room window, he had something.

When Irina came out to the kitchen to start her coffee a little while later, he was sitting at the dining table. Her steps slowed. She wasn't used to seeing him awake, let alone dressed, at this time.

"Mikhail, what is it?"

He heard the note of concern in her voice and realized that she must think something was truly wrong. Something more than just walking out on a live interview and effectively taking an acetylene torch to his acting career.

He rubbed at a stain on table. "I'm fine," he said. "Well, physically I'm fine. But. . . I screwed up."

His heart pounded as he filled her in on what had happened. He watched her face carefully, looking for signs that she was disappointed or angry with him.

Instead, his sister took everything in with remarkable calm.

"Okay," she said. "Now what?"

Fear spiked through him. The openness of that question, the possibilities of what could follow, terrified him in their enormity. It was like standing in an open airlock, preparing to step into the expanse of space for the first time. Or what he imagined that'd be like, being that he'd never been off planet.

He opened his mouth and then closed it again. He wanted to tell her his plan, but he was afraid of what she'd say. The Radnovskys had always been entertainers. Even Irina had acted at one time, before Kolya's condition demanded she take a job with better benefits.

Summoning his courage, he forced the words out. "There's a salvage outfit I heard about. Stalwart Corporation. They need more people to hire on to their crews." He paused. "There's a signing bonus. Plus, my pay."

He explained how he'd heard of people who signed on to these types of operations who built whole businesses on the side. Or digital products they sold when they reconnected to the main network at every resupply station. There was always downtime that could be put to good use.

"Even with the signing bonus, I won't make as much as I do now," he said. "Though hopefully I'll be able to generate some extra money on the side from odd jobs. I'll send some of it to you. Whatever you need."

Irina leaned back against the kitchen counter. She looked younger, the artificial light in the apartment blurring away some of the lines in her face.

"We'll manage," she said. "We'll have to. You can't keep doing what you're doing."

"Not now, anyway."

"Even before that. You haven't been happy for a long time."

True. Yet, he'd never dared to look around or think of changing jobs, for fear of losing the income. He'd used Kolya's condition like a crutch, too afraid to consider his own life seriously and acknowledge that maybe the family legacy wasn't meant for him anymore. Not in the same way.

The job description from Stalwart stated that the contract length was two years. That was a long time to be away from Telkeon. Yet it also meant a lot of time to amass the funds he'd need to make his own movies when he got back, with the kinds of scripts he wanted to see and roles he'd die to have. Things like *Moonlight in the Abyss*. Stories that mattered.

"I don't think grandfather would have wanted me to make things I hate," Radnovsky said.

She came across the kitchen and took his hand. "I don't think so either."

His pulse slowed, and the tension in his chest dissipated. If he did this, if he worked hard, he could be happy, and Irina and Kolya would be taken care of.

"I'll come back," he said. As much to convince her as himself.

"And we'll be waiting." Irina's smile was brighter than the first light of starrise. "Two hundred million people went to the frontier and built new worlds for themselves. Go make one for yourself, Mikhail. Find the story that's worth telling."

About the Author

Shannon Fox is a multi-genre writer of stories spanning past, present, and future. Her work often features morally gray characters doing their best in a complex world. Her short stories have appeared in several publications, and she has more work forthcoming this year from *DreamForge Anvil* and *Air and Nothingness Press*. One of her recent short stories was included in the *Monsters, Movies & Mayhem* anthology, edited by Kevin J. Anderson, which won a 2021 Colorado Book Award. She has a B.A. in Literature-Writing from UC-San Diego and owns a digital marketing company. Shannon grew up outside of Boulder, Colorado, in the shadow of the beautiful Flatirons.

*****~~~~~*****

Live From the Troll Factory

by Edward Barnfield

We need to be careful on cloudy days. Bright sun is the norm now, scorching and searing, but the boys are used to that. They strip to their underpants and let the sweat drip down their backs. Storms have lost their surprise, too. We cover things in plastic scraps and hunker in the dark, let the wind rip above us. The most recent squall gutted our last working jeepney, flung its hood half a mile down the track.

But clouds mean enforced quiet. The solar-panel-powered server grinds to a halt, which cuts off the internet, which means that no one can work. You have time to think, and nobody wants that.

Recently, Josh has taken to organising neighbourhood patrols during downtime. There are rumours of guerrillas marching from village to village, so we need to be prepared, he says.

"They'll be after our machines," he thunders. "Internet is just another scarce resource to fight over now."

I let him go, a figure from a dream. He looks too big in his bathrobe and beach shorts, his beard blending with his body hair, an unbroken grey-and-ginger rug running the length of him. His henchmen are all thin and cruel, the ones who pick fights when they've nothing else to do.

Donal is by my elbow.

"Nice tae see him putting yon inferior materials tae work," he says.

Donal is what was once called our webmaster. A native of Glasgow, he burns like paper in the Philippines heat. He is currently the crimson shade you only see in artificial flavouring, which means in a day he will be peeling off sheets of skin. He and Josh are the only other Westerners working on this project, which I suppose makes him my closest friend. Donal has always been quietly respectful towards me, presumably because I'm the only non-pixelated woman he sees.

"Aff tae update th' map," he says. "Got tae be enough ginger for that."

'Ginger' means juice means battery power. Donal is obsessed with tracking the dead zones of the internet, the environments too harsh for data to survive. He sends pings out around the world, waits for an echo, and transcribes the results in scrawling longhand.

I understand why. Without our fixations, all that is left is the job. Look at the boys, sleeping in the rumpus room, huddled like rats in a nest. They work for as long as the power holds, then crash for days in a heap.

I suppose this place is my obsession. I know the name of everyone who's worked here, keep a list of who quit and who remains, all those boys with the oddly assonant names. Rodrigo and Benigno, both snoring on a mat. Paulo and Piolo, who slipped away in the night. I chart how much food is left in the inventory, dip a measure into the buckets we use to collect rain.

The kitchen is all aftermath, splatters and stench and grey garlic smears. The primus stove in the corner, dry for weeks, reeks of undigestible food. I briefly consider cleaning it, weigh up what remains of our water supply, and then head to the roof to check on the pots.

It's hard to avoid the world from up here. First time I saw this view, everything was green and tangled, a vast wet jungle stretching out to the city's heat haze on the far horizon. Hard to believe we've fallen so fast.

. . .

When I met Josh, he was running workshops on presentation skills for businesspeople. He had one of those itinerant CVs that impressed the corporate types, and a PowerPoint he clearly knew by heart. There were sessions called 'Have a phrase that pays' and 'Choosing signal over noise.' He was large and loud, and people valued his time, or at least enjoyed the break from the norm he offered.

We talked during a smoke break, me with the pack of Silk Cut I swore was my last, him with some complex electrical device that vented smoke that smelled of buttermilk.

"Good session," I said.

"Great team," he replied, an accent honed at some long-ago fee-paying school. "Of course, none of you are doing what you want."

"Well, I mean—"

"Don't get me wrong. We're all saving until we pay off the mortgage or waiting until the youngest gets through college. That's our collective tragedy. Retirement dreams versus finite time."

I was younger then, more easily impressed. "You have an alternative, I suppose?"

He grinned, a slash of white veneers amongst all the facial grooming. He told me of his career as a government relations specialist in the economic flashpoints of the world. He'd been in Tokyo when that seemed like the future, then reinvented himself for Hong

Kong, then Shanghai then Dubai then Riyadh. He'd soaked up the money while the swell grew, then deftly stepped aside before the crash, he said. Now he was biding time, getting paid to patronise company boardrooms before putting his big plan into operation.

"What will that be?" I asked.

I could tell he was assessing me, weighing the value of my time. I had grown used to being overlooked, the fat, friendly spinster in the corner.

He said: "The Philippines. Next boom town. Filipinos spend more time online than anyone else in the world. They're educated, speak English, Spanish, Tamil, Punjabi, even some Korean. I'm going to recruit a battalion and put it to work."

"Doing what?"

He dropped the smoking device into his jacket, exhaled a plume of sweet fumes. Then he handed me a business card with raised lettering and a watermark.

"Give me a call to find out."

. . .

"Rise n' shine, lazy bairns. Suns oot, guns oot." I can hear Donal yelling from two floors down, clattering an empty kerosene can for a reveille. Someone has started the generator, and the wheezing, groaning mechanism adds to the chorus.

While I've been reminiscing, cloud cover breaks, and the world starts to warm again. The metal ladder is already hot to the touch, and any further delay in climbing down would give me blistered fingers. I take a last look before returning to the melee.

It's hard to describe the smell of the office after all this time. Think of brothers' bath towels in a soccer changing room. All around, the boys shamble and groan as they settle down to their workstations, wait for the achingly slow start-up.

It's ironic that the internet, the great circus of horrors that fuelled the climate crisis, should be its most public victim. Donal explained it to me once—the multifactor variants that brought it crashing to the ground. First were the energy costs, the server farms left to fry when they became economically unviable. Then America's West Coast dropped from the map, and 5,000 miles of copper cable drowned in acidic saltwater.

All that's left now are faint little pockets of survival, autonomous networks crawling along at glacial speeds, four colours, low resolution. Africa has done surprisingly well, the cheap NGO schemes and solar generators creating ideal conditions for subsistence, as have the dictatorships that walled themselves away, created private grids out of paranoia. Them, scavengers like us, a few communes in Europe and scientific outposts at the edge of the world. That's all that's left. That, and the silence.

Which makes for a poor online experience. Raised on the web, the boys can't handle the thin lines of code they're forced to work with. Rather than the infinite catalogue they grew up with, their soundtrack is a battery-operated boombox from before they were born. I try to limit their options to the classics—Nick Cave, Jarvis Cocker. Digital dance would only torture them with what they can't have.

Back in the day, these boys created whole personas through the internet. With the tools at their disposal, they built an online actors' studio, a repertory company of fake identities. Rodrigo masqueraded as an American physicist and assembled 650,000 followers, while Benigno ran popular pages of 'real science' content that infected actual newsfeeds.

You think how baroque it was—the astroturfing operations with fake company credentials, the endless looped arguments that ate through the oxygen. The hours people spent debating us, the energy.

Because the crisis has flattened that, simplified everything. The discourse only exists on a subsistence level now. There are message boards around the world, desperate for news and hope. We contact them with rumours of potable water or angry screeds accusing this neighbourhood or that tribe of hoarding resources. It is dumb, angry work, but it keeps the boys occupied.

I'm thinking on this, watching over my flock of bare-backed charges, when there is a shout from outside. The door crashes open, and a body is propelled through.

Josh has returned. With company.

. . .

I only really became aware of Josh's operation when my old firm started receiving regular invoices from Manila. We were a niche packaging engineering business, and life was as interesting as that sounds, so an overseas supplier seemed positively exotic. My manager was skittish when I asked why the seminar presenter from two years back was still getting paid. It was Janice, the new social media girl with the fraudulent CV, who explained it to me.

"He's brilliant," she said. "Manages whole online communities for us. Thousands of 'likes' for every post. We're the most popular industrial concern in the West Midlands because of him."

We had been facing criticism for a while over the cost and waste of all that plastic and paper. Swans were showing up dead in parks with branded packaging in their gullet. Josh's operation had been deployed to counter online criticism, and it seemed effective enough. I dug the business card out of my drawer.

I'm not sure what I expected when he flew me over for an interview. Flattered, I suppose, that he claimed to remember our conversation in the cold all those months ago. Suspicious also, anticipating some sad, middle-aged seduction technique or a room with a padlock on the outside. But you have to remember how bored I was, how disappointed with life's promises.

Piolo received me at the airport, immaculate in a shiny business suit I suspect had only seen funerals and weddings before. He called me ma'am, separated me from the package tourists and sex traffickers, and then we drove out into the jungle for five hours, talking all the way. I knew before I'd arrived that this was the job I wanted.

The office was immaculate, white walls, curved glass. It stood like a spacecraft down a dirt path, trees thick on either side. You would hear this tremendous rustling and see branches bend, and it would mean a troop of monkeys was descending, scattering over the roof and across the yard.

Most of the boys lived there, finishing their shifts and moving to the backroom, swapping their desktops for PlayStations. Josh encouraged it, blurring the boundaries of labour and play, and holding exuberant parties every Friday to celebrate completed targets or new recruits.

My title was General Manager, but I was really Den Mother, making sure the boys ate, sorting out their problems. I felt enormous tenderness for them, fresh out of college and high school, excited to put their talents to work. They called each other 'Kabayan,' and, after a while, I felt like a kabayan too.

There was always a distinctly freelance element to our work. Josh was very protective of client confidentiality and never told us where the money was coming from. Inevitably, given the mood of the time, most of the activity centred around environmental concerns. The boys were encouraged to intervene in any online argument they could find, to always take the side of the corporations.

"We're defence lawyers, boys," Josh would say. "Everyone has the right to an impassioned advocate." I think he meant 'dispassionate' or 'impartial', but I didn't like to contradict him.

I had qualms. There was a lot of targeted doxing going on, shadowy government work you could get away

131

with out here. We'd report people to their employers and catfish activists' locations. Donal was always testing new software that found pungent details in bank accounts and personal email. Still, the mood of the office was always light. There was a lot of laughter. It didn't seem like we were hurting anyone.

It was easy, in the jungle, to ignore the unravelling of the world. I found myself ignoring messages from home, even as the exclamation marks multiplied in the subject lines. I had found purpose, I told myself. That part of my life was over.

By the time we saw the smoke, it was too late to panic. The disasters caught the attention—the floods, the fires, the sheer randomness that displaced whole cities. But it was the aggregate that was truly terrifying—the infrastructure unable to withstand heatwaves, the service crews blocked from reaching bridges before they warped, which stopped vital deliveries, which collapsed food systems. Whole communities strangled by supply chains.

We kept typing. When the great social networks crashed, the boys seemed seized by a particular sort of militancy, determined to change the conversation through sheer force of will. They would argue on internet forums for displaced people, accuse bereaved families of being crisis actors. Josh was at the heart of it. He'd always been loud, but now he seemed driven, animated by a sort of perpetual motion. The old playfulness drained away. He sent boys into the courtyard to catch the passing monkeys, armed them with slingshots and sticks.

"We win the argument or accept extinction," he bellowed. "Choose to win."

Some of the kabayan began crying in the night.

. . .

I realise I am the only person still sitting after a few moments. The body is on the ground, and everyone else is around it like a tight square at a barn dance. The bullies form the inner ring, while my keyboard warriors, my boys, jostle around the edges. Proximity seems to raise the temperature of the room, sweat on my neck and in my eyes.

The throng parts for Josh Meadows, former fellow of the British Investors' League. There is dirt on his face and in his beard, and two jagged lines on the back of his hand, blistering with blood. He's clearly winded.

"We have. . . a traitor in our midst, boys," he says, angling on a desk to catch his breath.

One of the thinner thugs, Enrique, grabs a handful of hair and pulls the body's head back. It is Piolo. Stripped of his wedding suit, half his previous size, but puppy fat enough around the cheeks for me to recognise him. A lavender bruise on his left temple.

Benigno, who Piolo mentored in his first weeks, aims a solid kick through the wall of legs. Gentle, smiley Donal is sharing loud opinions on strangulation and castration.

"Tak' him ootside," he yells. "String him up."

Too many hands drag Piolo's small form through the office and out the back. I catch just a glimpse of his face—jaw slack, eyes dull, as though he'd abandoned the luxury of protest out there in the wild. As Josh walks past, I reach out and grab the dirty towelling of his bathrobe.

"What's he supposed to have done, Josh?"

He looks almost stricken by my question. "Breach of contract," he says.

They won't allow me to attend the interrogation. Rodrigo, who I nursed through a nasty bout of e-coli back in April, bars my way and says, "No women allowed," as though the plural even exists for us anymore.

I busy myself in the kitchen, trying to make a dent with the last threads of steel wool. By the time I've cleared a patch of metal on the stove, the shouting has faded, and I can hear Josh as he preens and monologues. I think of his old PowerPoints, the urgent graphics, the emphatic text. No need for that anymore.

After the Gold Rush

At some point, the boys start taking turns to beat on their victim. You hear them build to a crescendo as someone takes a run-up for a punch or kick, and then a collective roar as the blow lands. They tire of that after a while, and all that is left are wet thuds and groans.

I'm still working on the sink when they file back in, looking lost and drained. I will learn later that Piolo told them, under significant duress, that he'd been walking for days out there. That the jungle is mostly black and dry now, like a lunar surface. That he'd made it as far as the next town before turning back, convinced there was nothing left that could resemble a rescue.

After a while, they go back online. Donal retreats to the backroom, tries to map the last signs of life. Josh goes into his office, locks the door. Benigno finds a working community link landing somewhere in Uganda, but then his screen hangs, then goes black.

It dawns on me then that the last word on the internet will be a lie, typed by a boy who doesn't know better. Not because he necessarily believes it, but because of the superiority that comes from misleading others. That's all we want, as a people. To know there is someone worse off than ourselves.

Piolo is still in the courtyard. I look out of the window, try to assess if he's breathing, but the angle and the haze make it impossible to judge.

I'll go out there later, when the boys take a break, and the sun is not so fierce. One way or another, it's my mess to clear up.

###

About the Author

Edward Barnfield is a writer and researcher living in the Middle East. His stories have appeared in Ellipsis

Zine, Lunate, Strands, Janus Literary, Leicester Writes, Cranked Anvil, and Reflex Press, among others. He's on Twitter at @edbarnfield

*****~~~~~*****

The Front of the Pack

by Lauren C. Teffeau

"We want a name," Agent Donaldson demanded in a voice like a hatchet, blunt and decisive. "Give us that, and your involvement in all this will be. . . overlooked."

Even if the deal turned out to be bogus, the bureau must have been desperate to offer anything approaching immunity. Landis adjusted his shirtsleeves, thumb hovering over the cool surface of his new cufflink made of polished ceramic. It wasn't a nervous gesture on his part, but Agent Donaldson took it that way based on the arrogant tilt of her head in the direction of the one-way mirror on the far wall of the interrogation room.

He understood what she and whoever else was watching on thought they saw: a middleman with pretensions for more, given his rumpled bespoke suit and designer dress shoes, desperate to cut a deal at the first sign of difficulty. Fools. He knew better than anyone the longer he stayed in this business, the harder it was to keep your nose clean. By that logic, this meeting was long overdue. But Agent Donaldson's first mistake was assuming the nearest safe house would be sufficient when they picked him up on his way out of a lunch meeting downtown with a prospective client.

"As I already told you, I'm a freelancer, facilitating, shall we say, *unique* transactions for a wide variety of buyers and sellers with utmost discretion."

Agent Donaldson pushed a lock of salt-and-pepper hair behind her ear. "Last October, you *facilitated* the purchase of ten acres in Turkmenistan to a biotechware company now accused of atrocious human rights violations at the facility there."

"What the buyers choose to do with their property is neither my concern nor my responsibility."

Donaldson pounded the table with the meat of her fist. "Then there's the cargo containers of bonobos bound for Mexico that had been injected with unauthorized, highly experimental antibiotics."

"Clearly, in that instance, the supplier misrepresented the condition of the goods in question. An unfortunate cost of doing business, I'm afraid."

"A likely story," Agent Donaldson said, not bothering to hide her sneer. "Then, how do you explain the associated medical waste that was also found on board?"

Landis shrugged. "The shipping manifest must have been falsified. I never—"

"*Please.* Let's not forget all the violations you've racked up over the years." She ticked them off on her fingers. "Possession of potential biological weapon components and illegal military prototypes, patent infringements, intellectual property theft, dumping on public lands."

He swallowed back a surprised laugh at the last one. Since when had the government been truly interested in tackling industrial pollution? Certainly not in his lifetime.

"Never proven." Or easily settled. Eventually. "You know none of those cases ever saw trial."

Nevertheless, she was trying to establish a pattern of behavior, intimidate him by demonstrating all that they knew. That they *thought* they knew. Too bad she couldn't yet see the forest for the trees.

"It's only a matter of time before we unravel your underground research network." She folded her hands behind her back with a triumphant curl to her mouth. "Either give up your superiors or spend the rest of your life behind bars."

Landis chuckled at her utter lack of imagination. That was her second mistake: Jail wasn't a threat for someone like him. If anything, it demonstrated just how important his work was.

"We know what kind of man you are," she continued, as she began to pace back and forth with performative deliberation. "When IRB regulations or industry standards get in the way, your organization is there to keep R&D going regardless of laws, legalities, and basic human decency." Her dander rose with each word. "When drug trials fail, researchers go to you to recruit test subjects too desperate to make a fuss. If scientists need dangerous compounds for their experiments, you're the ones who smuggle them into the country, granting a veneer of legitimacy to the transactions. A facility in the middle of nowhere, away from prying eyes? No problem. A place to dump toxic materials or tapped out lab subjects? You've got just the thing."

She didn't mention the global network of financiers that supported them or the hackers and hit teams who covered their tracks, but it didn't seem especially politic to bring it up while she was on a roll.

"If I'm guilty of all these things—not that I am, of course, but if I were—have you ever wondered why there's a demand for such services?"

She spun on her heel to face him, her contempt plain. "All I know is, you're a greedy son of a bitch."

139

He sighed. Definitely lacking in imagination. She straightened her blazer, involuntarily glancing at the one-way mirror on the wall. Whoever was watching needed to hear this too. "If a shadowy cottage industry supporting illegal research does exist, perhaps it's because we've forgotten what it means to *really* advance. The Golden Quarter—when our scientists were *allowed* to make mistakes, sometimes catastrophically so, in pursuit of greatness—was a long damn time ago."

Landis was hardly the only person who noticed how their so-called scientific prowess, their potential for *more*, had been hamstrung for decades now by unreasonable regulations and public discourse that reveled in humanity's capacity for ignorance and manufactured outrage. So he had decided to do something about it by identifying industries and innovations that were desperate to escape the red tape and take a step forward for the good of humankind. A lofty goal that would have been celebrated in a previous era.

He grimaced. Now was not the time for ego but education. "Scientific achievements—I'm not talking about incremental bullshit that gets churned out in journals, but real breakthroughs—require risks. Risks the ivory tower, funding agencies, corporate whistleblowers, and the general public simply no longer tolerate."

Landis leaned back in his chair, suppressing the urge to inspect his cufflinks again. "Now," he said in a calmer voice, "I'm not saying that's what I do, but wouldn't it follow that certain mechanisms pop up to exploit such obvious limitations to scientific inquiry?"

Agent Donaldson shook her head in disbelief. "You not only run a clearinghouse for illegal research, you're a true believer?" She rolled her eyes. "How noble."

"I *believe* that you have to break a few eggs to make an omelet." He put his elbows on the table and marveled again that the security measures hadn't picked up the miniature EMP prototype in his cufflinks. When

Dr. Williams approached Landis to secure overseas funding, he'd been skeptical about the composite ceramic's shielding properties. But you couldn't argue with results. Or the generous finder's fee.

"Unlike the government," Landis continued, "we aren't afraid of real progress. Of making the hard calls to keep us advancing. We're the ones ripping the lid off Pandora's Box so you don't have to." After all, the bureau was always happy to confiscate any new technology they came across to reverse-engineer in their laboratories. He shrugged, an elegant lift of his shoulders. "You should be thanking us, really, for being the bad guys in the PR narratives that placate the public."

"All you've done is turned research into a weapon."

He tipped his head, pretending to consider that. "Respectfully, this country's forgotten that research has always been a weapon. It's only those who get out in front of the pack who can actually wield it."

With that, he depressed the button on his cufflink. A half-second later, the fluorescent lights overhead wavered, then shut off completely. Emergency LEDs strobed across the room in the moment that followed, while ominous creaks and metallic whines echoed throughout the rest of the facility as the power cut out.

Agent Donaldson glanced about. "Wait here."

"I think not." Landis smoothly rose to his feet. Her third mistake was not handcuffing him while she had the chance.

She pulled out her sidearm. "Another step, and I'll shoot."

How utterly predictable. "You'll find your gun doesn't recognize your handprint anymore," he said casually.

"What?" She tried to fire, but the trigger wouldn't comply. "How did you—"

Landis approached the door. "After all your intel, do you really have to ask?"

He supposed she did, as he left her sputtering. It would take time to override the handprint lockout to use the manual trigger. Same for every guard in the facility that had rejected their untraceable, all-cash offer to look the other way as he sauntered past the security gate.

Unopposed, he walked out of the building and into a waiting sedan. They still had no idea what they were up against. The world didn't stop just because one country had become complacent. A hard lesson. Only time would tell if they had wit enough to see it.

In the meantime, he had arrangements to make. He outlined the cufflink with the tip of his thumbnail. They were going to love this little beauty in Asia, and of course Dr. Williams would need support to move into the production phase after such a flawless demonstration.

Luckily Landis knew just who to call.

###

About the Author

Lauren C. Teffeau is a speculative fiction writer based in New Mexico. Her novel, *Implanted* (Angry Robot, 2018), mashing up cyberpunk, solarpunk, adventure, and romance, was shortlisted for the 2019 Compton Crook award for best first SF/F/H novel. Her short fiction can be found in a variety of professional and semi-pro magazines and anthologies.

*****~~~~~*****

Last Bite at the Klondike

by Liam Hogan

Grigor floated awkwardly into the cavernous mess hall, cradling something under one arm, pulling on the straps of the walls and ceiling with the other. I looked up—or was it down?—from the bench I was Velcroed to, a spark of curiosity banishing my sour mood as I swallowed what I'd been chewing.

"What's that?"

He waggled the bottle, then hugged it to his chest like it was a baby. "Fifty-year-old whisky. *Cask* strength."

"Jackpot!" I tapped my watch; just under two hours to go. The table in front of me was littered with the very best the solar system had to offer, from Wagyu burgers to slivers of something vat-grown and fishy that apparently cost an arm and a leg back on Earth. I'd grown bored of it all, repulsed by the obscene waste. A whisky older than I was, though. . . "Well, bring it on over," I said. "We'll make a dent in it, at least before we have to leave."

"Shall I be mother?" He grinned and began the complicated process of transferring the priceless whisky to two sipping pouches. Not that it mattered if some of it floated away in zero-g, not now. Except it would be utterly criminal to waste *any* of it.

Time was, this hall would have been packed with up to a hundred prospectors, begging for a taste. Chaotic and noisy as hell. But *fun*. Now it was a ghost town, a graveyard. A wake, with just two mourners in attendance.

We would be the last to depart, the gold rush officially over. The only reason we were still up here was because we'd sacrificed safety for weight, desperate to fill every last inch of the *Betsey's* hold before the Klondike, and us, were forever out of range.

Grigor handed me my pouch, and I clinked it against his. It didn't make any noise, so I had to say the *clink* bit myself. Depending on where you stood, the coincidences of us being, at that moment, in the hollowed belly of a giant asteroid, sipping rare Scottish single malt, were so numerous as well as preposterous that they risked tripping over each other. It all started with the Chinese comet sample return mission that failed its most important and earliest step: *First, catch your comet.* Left drifting through the empty void of the cosmos, looking for alternative science to do, it was pure luck it spotted the hurtling asteroid in time to bring its spectrometer to bear.

It was that analysis that earned the Manhattan-sized chunk of space debris the unofficial name of *Klondike,* initially nothing more than an astronomical curiosity, an attention-grabbing headline on the 'net. The Chinese were quick to claim ownership even so—*finders keepers*—but the International Space Agency lay down the law: the only bits of an asteroid that belonged to anyone were those successfully returned either to Earth, or to Earth orbit. That was the ruling that kicked off the gold rush.

Last Bite at the Klondike

Technically, the Klondike was only something like a thousandth of one percent gold, even if the cartoonists back on Earth depicted it as a giant gold nugget. A giant gold nugget heading *straight* down Earth's throat, or close enough. The comet chaser had calculated its trajectory and given it a seventy-two percent chance of collision. And even if it wasn't quite the dinosaur killer, it was plenty big enough to ruin a *lot* of dinner parties and to send humankind scurrying back to the Stone Age. Half a billion Hiroshimas, give or take. Big enough to make global warming look like a sniffle, especially if it resulted in an impact winter, as it well might, depending on where it made land.

So the ISA lay down another law: all asteroid mining missions, whether Chinese, European, American or privately funded, must work together to nudge the Klondike onto a safer path. One where it would pass by, on current predictions, at a breezy fifty thousand kilometres. Close, but no smoking crater.

Though if Grigor and I didn't leave in time, we'd be passing by with it. Because that was another thing, the unlikeliest of coincidences that made it all happen. Mining the speeding Klondike would have been impossible, given simple planetary mechanics, if what we were busy mining wasn't already pointed roughly at the Earth. All we had to do, once the valuable elements were extracted and refined, was to slow them down enough so that a shuttle could ferry them to terra firma, in the case of the rare earths the Earth was crying out for, or we could leave them in orbit, in the case of the iron and nickel that was in the way of the good stuff.

All of this stopped being possible the instant the Klondike drew level with the Earth (at a safe distance) and then started zooming away from it. Well before that, actually, our heavily laden spaceship would have to work flat out to also not zoom away along with the asteroid. Most of the miners, and their ships, had left at the sweet

145

spot, the point at which the journey to the rapidly approaching Earth was shortest, and needed the least fuel. No such luck for us late arrivals. There was a limit to the acceleration the *Betsey*, and more importantly, meat-sack astrominers, could endure. That point of no return, in both space and time, was rapidly approaching.

We asteroid miners talked a lot about a thing called a gravity tax. It's why Grigor was handing me a refilled pouch containing even more of the fifty-year-old whisky and not something less aged and far cheaper, as we both silently toasted all those many miners who were no longer with us. Because the overall cost, pretty much, was the same; getting anything into space made it instantly more precious than gold.

Delivering tonnes of high-grade building material to low Earth orbit, to make the next generation of space stations, or even to the new Apollo Lunar Base, was therefore *valuable*, though it really only covered the day-to-day ruinous costs of running a mining operation in space. There wasn't any particular profit in iron or nickel. Or even, as it happened, in gold. Stuff the Earth had plenty of, if not exactly where the space industry needed it. It was the rarer stuff we were after, the europium, terbium, neodymium, praseodymium, and rhodium, the things we needed to make the best batteries, magnets, lasers, and superconductors, all the things to march us into a brighter, greener future. Gold was better than nothing, but no jackpot—the more we returned, the cheaper it became.

When people realised that any bonanza was going to be short-lived, a whole raft of Longitude Act worthy ideas were conjured up to try and extend it. Some of them turned out to be semi-practical. Like the rail-guns that would continue to fire long after we'd left, trading momentum with the asteroid to shoot valuable pellets of refined ore at a designated crater on the moon, where it could be retrieved in the future once the Klondike stopped its firing, out of range or out of bullets. Some crazies suggested we should scale that up wholesale, nudge the Klondike to collide with our nearest neighbour, an effective way of killing its troubling momentum. And, wiser heads quickly pointed out, everyone on the moon, as well as, with the kicked up, high velocity, lunar and asteroid rubble, a fair percentage of those in Earth orbit and even possibly some of those down on Earth.

Plans to hollow out the Klondike, to transform it into a second moon, to be mined at leisure as it orbited the Earth, ignored just how much energy as well as time that would take. Though, hollowed out it had been, on a smaller scale. Our mining ships were cramped things, packed with equipment. Uncomfortable living spaces. But, as the mining robots chased veins of valuable ore, they opened up tunnels and caverns, and it had been pretty easy to turn them into airtight chambers for habitation, like the mess hall, the workshops, and the many cabins.

Spaces that now resembled the Marie Celeste. The gravity tax worked both ways and getting something down to Earth, safely anyway, was fuel costly, especially if it started out travelling at Klondike speeds. However personal your possessions might be, they weren't worth a fraction of the rare, rare earths you could carry in their place instead, so they'd all been left behind, abandoned wherever they last lay, from clothes to chess sets to untapped supplies of food and drink. That was how Grigor had managed to scrounge an unopened fifty-year-old malt from one of the abandoned miner's quarters.

We'd be taking nothing back with us except ore, most of it already refined by the Klondike's three nuclear reactors to make it as pure and hence valuable, pound for pound, as possible. The reactors, of course, were themselves fuelled by uranium we'd carved out of the asteroid, and we used their excess energy to split any water we recovered to make our rocket fuel for the journey home.

147

My watch beeped at me. It had always been a race to see which arrived first, the point it became impossible to escape the Klondike and return to Earth, or the point the Betsey's hold was full. In the end, the robots stacking ingots of metal and containers of powdered rare earths had won that race; the Betsey's capacity had been reached a scant fifteen minutes before we absolutely had to leave. Pretty close to a dead heat. We really ought to be down there already, running system checks, duplicating what the AIs would already have done, far more efficiently.

"Last orders," I announced with a hiccup, unstrapping myself from the table and pushing clumsily towards the walls. "C'mon. Time to go."

"I'm not coming," Grigor said, still sat there, grinning pleasantly.

"*What?*" I tried to rack my brains. What had we just been talking about? Future plans and things we were looking forward to most, back on Earth. And then I realised, stupidly, belatedly, it had all been *me*. I'd rabbited on as usual, not noticing how quiet Grigor was, mere grunts of what I'd taken as assent.

Grigor decanted the last of the whisky into his pouch. Had we really drunk that much? A whole bottle between us? No wonder I was feeling woozy. Good thing I wasn't driving.

"I've got everything I need, right here." Grigor waved his meaty hand around the empty hall. "Food, water, power, air enough for at least two decades."

"But. . . "

"And *work*. I can help keep the mining operation going. You know I can."

I did. The very first mining consortiums to land on the Klondike had been fully automated, AI and robots. They hadn't been a success. Perhaps, if another Klondike came along, they'd do better, having learnt from the many failures, the unpredictabilities of any mining venture. But right now, a combined man/machine mission was the best option. We were engineers, strictly, rather than miners. We kept the drills and refineries going, solving the problems they—or anyone—hadn't encountered before.

"But what's the point?" I said, as my watch bleeped incessantly at me. I silenced it. If he really wasn't leaving, I had an extra eighty kilos of allowance, and therefore an extra few minutes to talk him out of it. Though, if he took too long to change his mind, we could end up in a heap of trouble. I flicked through a couple of the alternative scenarios the AI was giving me, still assuming a crew of two. Mostly, it would mean leaving precious ore behind, and suffering a far longer, slower ride back to Earth. I groaned.

"You ever heard of the interstellar spaceship paradox?" Grigor said, as if time wasn't that important. "The one that says you never leave?"

"Um, no?"

"The logic goes something like this. You build a spaceship, a big one, but it takes a thousand years to get to its destination. Meanwhile, technology back on Earth races on. Better reactors, better drives. When you launch another ship, ten years later, it quickly overtakes the first, and arrives a century earlier. So you shouldn't have launched the first one, right?"

"*Right. . .* " My head hurt. Grigor had always been friendly, but I'd never considered him garrulous. That was why his silence as I rambled on earlier hadn't rung any alarm bells. Now, it seemed he was trying to bend my brain into a whisky-soaked pretzel.

"But a ship launched twenty years later, overtakes that second ship. So you shouldn't launch that one, either."

"And so on?"

"And so on," he agreed.

I nodded, then shook my head. "What has this to do with you, staying on this rock?"

He shrugged. "Maybe nothing. Maybe everything. I'll be the furthest from the Earth anyone has ever been.

Even if it's only a small, one-way step, it's still a step. Someone has to take it. And I've got, what, ten, fifteen years of my life left? No wife, no family. No particular desire for either, even if it were still possible. So, why not me?"

Was he talking about his age? I thought of the lead underpants some miners fashioned. The asteroid was low-level radioactive, just like everything else. You were more at a risk from cosmic radiation on the way here. Once you were in the caverns, you were pretty well shielded. But that six-month journey from Earth was plenty damaging.

"Sure, but back home, you'll at least be rich."

"Not me," he grunted. "My stake, already sold." He swept an arm at the banquet I'd been picking at. "I won't be rich like *this* rich. Here, I can live like a king."

I blinked. Already sold? The fool. "But there's no company. . . "

He snorted at that.

". . . and no rescue, if things go wrong. With the Klondike, or with you."

"So be it."

I frowned. He'd obviously thought this through, which put him at a distinct advantage. I was pretty sure I ought to be able to argue he was being an idiot, but that probably wouldn't be enough to make him change his mind. And I didn't really have the time. I briefly considered trying to knock him out, manhandle him to the *Betsey*, but Grigor weighed twenty kilos more than I did, and if he was grizzled, he was still a bear of a man.

"You sure?" I said. My last argument. Because you can only change your mind while there's more than one option.

"I'm sure. Go on, get out of here."

I didn't hesitate any longer, breaking several records for reaching the cargo bay, especially when drunk. Suiting up felt like it took forever, but at last I was strapped into the pilot's seat aboard the Betsey, the co-pilot position yawningly empty, stabbing a finger down on the release button, the one I might as well have re-labelled "Are *you* sure?"

The takeoff was rough as hell. It was always going to be. The magnetic launch system accelerated the *Betsey* at a peak of 15 gees, and only the pressurised space suit stopped all my blood pooling in the wrong places and me blacking out. All to fling me violently away from the Klondike, flung backwards, though still travelling forwards relative to the Earth, but at a speed low enough that we ought to be able to still make orbit, to rendezvous with one of the ever-expanding orbitals. After unloading the raw building materials for their next growth spurt, I'd refuel just enough for Earth re-entry, carrying a conservatively estimated billion dollars worth of rare elements, future electronics.

My cut would be much less than that. Not enough to afford wagyu, or aged whisky, not on a regular basis anyway. But enough to finally retire, if I wanted to. Enough to buy a small place, somewhere not too crowded, somewhere still considered remote. There, I could install a big old telescope, and watch the crowded night skies, knowing that, somewhere up there, beyond the thousands of micro-satellites, each controlled by Klondike-sourced electronics, a crazy space miner was still sat all alone on the mother of all lodes. Knowing that I could have been there with him, at the outer edges of the solar system, if only I had the guts.

I hope he unearths another bottle of whisky or two to keep him company, and that he remembers me in his prayers.

###

About the Author

Liam Hogan is an award-winning short story writer, with stories in *Best of British Science Fiction* and in *Best of British Fantasy* (NewCon Press). He's been published by *Analog, Daily Science Fiction,* and Flame Tree Press, among others. He helps host Liars' League London, volunteers at the creative writing charity, Ministry of Stories, and lives and avoids work in London. More details can be found at his blog, http://happyendingnotguaranteed.blogspot.co.uk

*****~~~~~*****

All Our Signs Align

by Eve Morton

At first, teaching the aliens sign language was a suitable challenge for Gregory. Growing up with Deaf parents, while he had hearing, meant that he already felt as if he was in two worlds. He spoke out loud during the day in school, sharing secrets and stories without the use of his hands to his friends and teachers. Then, at home, he'd sink into silence and translate his day into something that his parents—a stern, older couple who had had Gregory late in their life—could understand and comprehend. Sometimes, he'd need to come up with his own forms of signs to translate the new world to his parents into something beyond spelling words out with his fingers. Like when he understood that he was gay and wanted to introduce his new boyfriend to them, or when the scientists made first contact with aliens from another world, and no one on the news had close captioned the experience. Gregory fumbled with both events, hands shaking and wondering if his message was reading properly, but there was nothing to worry about.

His parents signed back, *I understand. I love you. And everything is going to be all right.*

Like some magic spell, one that always made him feel better when he was young, Gregory's parents' signed words spoke the truth. And so, Gregory was loved by them no matter what his sexuality, and even the alien invasion turned out to be a peaceful affair.

Gregory was no longer with Steven when the aliens came, but he had been casually seeing a man he'd met in his first year English Literature class. They'd both been reading *War of the Worlds* in bed, bodies lying opposite one another on the same thin twin mattress, and when the news first broke on their devices, they thought it was a joke. An Orson Welles type of experiment gone awry. Then, realizing that no one else in this large world of over eight billion people knew they were reading H. G. Wells together, they took the news seriously and acted accordingly by making out until their fear subsided.

When Gregory spoke next, he also signed, though Jeff was a hearing man; it was as if he understood the imperative to always speak in two languages at once now that alien life forms were here. After informing his parents what was going on, and then signing that he loved this boy with him—too soon, as it turned out for their still very new relationship—he dropped out of his English Literature classes and enrolled in Translation Studies.

Within five years, with another five boyfriends behind him, he was translating his American Sign Language into Alien Sign Language, the initials ASL taking on new meaning in a global and now intergalactic world.

His first classroom was on a starship that orbited around the new colony that had been discovered. It was yet another position between two worlds, familiar and comforting, and Gregory fell into the rhythm of teaching the aliens and other human translators quite happily. When the aliens presented with only three digits on their hands, he modified the alphabet to accommodate them. When they came to him with new concepts, such as *consciousness-trading* and *ineffable-happiness*, he struggled to find ways of expressing it to the humans around him, then on his five-fingered hands, and then to give the aliens back a sign they all could use to understand one another. When finally, after nearly six months of struggle, one of their six eyes lit up with the joy of comprehension, it was the best feeling Gregory had had in some time. Not since boyfriend number 5 kissed him under the moonlight filtered in from a spaceship. Finally, he'd met his biggest challenge so far. Humans and aliens could speak together, they could understand one another through their hands and bodies and faces, even if it was all so very different from each other.

So, when the government cancelled the sign language program, Gregory didn't understand. Hadn't things been going so well? What were they to do with this new language, one that had bloomed into an ever-expanding lexicon between the races after that first translation hurdle? When Gregory was called into his boss's office, and Sherry informed him of the new invention of a universal translator implant and free-form box that could be attached to a larynx of every human and every alien creature—so there was no need to share words any longer—he remained silent with his mouth, but his hands were lively with his true thoughts. He cursed. He cried out. He signed his frustration and skepticism at how something technological could replace the human-alien field of translation.

"You've been signing," Sherry said, her brows furrowed. "But I don't know what you're saying."

It was hard to believe that after all this time his boss still had not picked up even the most basic annoyance in someone's fingers. "It doesn't matter," Gregory said, and put his hands behind his back, where they still twitched with his anger. "I just don't understand

155

how a piece of technology can replace human and alien conversation and relationships."

"It translates for us now. We have the words."

"But language is about more than just words. It's those relationships that matter."

"It uses those relationships. The tech is based in AI, which has now scanned enough of the aliens' language, cultural documents, history, and stories to have a complete lexicon on which to draw its translations. Now there is no need for a shared language, the bridge sign you've been teaching. I'm sorry, but we simply don't need it anymore."

"AI?" he repeated, knowing the term but still not grasping how it could replace human touch. She gave him the basics—"artificial intelligence is sort of like robotics, where we can use the computational technology at our fingertips to create a whole database of definitions and translations, so the need for your skills is obsolete"— before he interrupted, "But what about concepts? Idioms?"

"What about them?"

"There is no direct translation for something like 'Once in a Blue Moon' in English, or 'Once in a Black Moon' for their language. We have different social constructs, different family and gender relationships, even different relationships to time and space. We have different fingers and hands, too. With all of this in mind, we've still made it so ASL combines our shared understanding into a shared language. Unless these translator boxes can also work together, rather than simple scanning, I fail to see how one can replace the other."

Sherry nodded as if she understood, but when she repeated her stance on AI, the wonderful ways in which this computer program had scanned and memorized all the alien cultures, Gregory stopped arguing. A long time ago, when he was only fingerspelling and not using the words of their sign language, his father had told him that the brain was a processing machine, not a memorization machine. *Stop trying to memorize me and talk with me instead.* The words had changed his approach to language, to understanding, and as he taught the new ASL to his human and alien students, and then learned from them, he remembered his father's stance more and more. He wanted to tell these words to Sherry now, but she would not believe them.

Even if she did, the decision had been made. There would be no ASL workers and interpreters and teachers any more. Their shared language would fade away as a cultural idiosyncrasy, something too ambitious like Esperanto, or something as foolish as Pig Latin.

In Gregory's last class on the starship, to a mixture of both alien and human students, he explained with his words in English and then in Alien Sign Language what had happened. The faces that stared back at him, no matter the color or texture of the skin or how many eyes they had, were filled with the same irrefutable sadness. They all agreed that the AI technology could not do what they had done together over these hard months, and all despaired that the language they had used together would fade away into nothing.

"But what happens to our names?" one of the aliens signed with zir three fingers. Zie had been adamant about no longer using fingerspelling for people's names; zie had come up with zir own moniker when zie reached a particular molting period in zir species' growth cycle, and zie had decided that a new name fit zir's new body that much better. Zie held up two fingers on zir hand, spelling out X, then Y, and then R; zie then held those fingers into a wave pattern to signal the final sign of zir's name. Gregory had always heard this name as *Zephyr*, the god of the wind, in his own mind, and he liked the way it danced in the alien's hands. "What if the translation box doesn't give me what I know I'm called?" zie asked.

"I know your name. We know your name. I hope it can be enough to hear it and see it one last time," Gregory said. He held up the letter G in ASL with his hand, and then brought it to his mouth. His name.

The other students, human and alien alike, followed with their own names. Gregory watched as everyone used the same language, the same shared understanding to signal how unique and wonderful they all were. A contraction, maybe—if they were all unique and wonderful, how could anyone be different?—but it didn't matter. They signed their names. They said their names out loud, if they could, and then the room grew quiet.

"I'm sorry," Gregory said in English and simultaneously signed to his classroom. "I don't know what else to say other than I'm so sorry. This is our last official class."

"But unofficially?" one of the humans asked, and also signed as he spoke. "Unofficially, we can do what we want, yes? We could meet at someone's house. We could keep talking, keep writing, keeping signing."

Gregory was struck by this suggestion. The starship he'd lived in for so long, orbiting and without grounding, made him think that homes were floating. Fleeting. The man, whose name was Abraham, went on to describe how they could all set up a foundation, a location, a library of some kind on the alien's planet and on earth. "We can keep talking, even if no one hears us." He laughed, seeming to understand his incidental pun. "I mean—"

"I know what you mean." Gregory added the pun in ASL so the others would get it. And they laughed, the way they could laugh, and they gestured with the shared laughing sign together.

"We can do that, yes," Gregory said. "We should do that. It reminds me of something my father said, actually. The brain is a processing machine, not a memorization machine. Our words are much the same.

They are about us, about the people, not a translation device."

"Yes," Abraham said. "I understand that. Do you all?"

The class clapped in their shared understanding, each silent and vocal word taking Gregory's breath away, like the announcement of the aliens and his own emergent sexuality once had.

And so they spent the rest of the time they had together planning and talking and signing some more. Gregory had come to his classroom full of melancholy and malaise, giving up his life's work for something that a bot could do now, but he left it, over an hour later, with a feeling of purpose. He still had a translation job with the government and intergalactic station; it would now be switched to a tech-focused section, and he'd be given new training, but even that drudgery took on new life if it meant he had a meeting room to go to on the alien world or on his home world, to keep speaking the language they had created together.

Gregory was about to lock up the classroom when he noticed that Abraham was still in the room. Though they were both human, both with five fingers and perfectly functioning ears and mouths for speech, they continued to speak to one another with their hands and using the alien signs between their regular words.

"You're still here. Are you okay?"

"I'm fine. I was just wondering what you were doing later on?"

"For work?"

"No, silly," Abraham said, and used Gregory's name with the diminutive silly term, rather than the insult term silly. When he smiled, Gregory remembered something else he'd not yet taught his class with his hands. Love, the kind of love between two people, no matter the sex and no matter the species, that could transcend everything. It had not been in the school curriculum

159

before, and since the aliens shared a different concept of love depending on their molting seasons, the international space agency didn't want to deal with it. And for a time, Gregory had been too busy to remember that side of his body, his heart, and his language. He'd focused on work.

But now, as Abraham stepped closer to him, and asked with his mouth this time—without using words—what they could do together, he filled with ideas. Their kiss became a caress, a hug, became something more between their bodies. When they pulled apart, they held hands, and an electric charge went through them.

"There's so much to say," Gregory said, and then shook his head. "A complete other world."

"Yes, that's true." Abraham held up Gregory's hands. He kissed the tip of his index finger, then his middle, then the ring, and the pinky before he folded the thumb into the center. He made nonsense spaces and syllables with his hand, a start to something else. "But I think you can handle it."

Gregory nodded. He was, after all, used to living in two worlds. Maybe now, as he kissed Abraham once again, he could also love in two worlds.

###

About the Author

Eve Morton is a writer living in Ontario, Canada. She teaches university and college classes on media studies, academic writing, and genre literature, among other topics. Her speculative work has appeared in *Strange Horizons, Star*Lines*, and *Eye to the Telescope*. Her latest book is *The Serenity Nearby*, released in 2022 by Sapphire Books. Find more information at authormorton.wordpress.com

*****~~~~~*****

Facing Reality
by Yelena Crane

On bad days, Logan wondered what right he had to save others from their VR addictions when he couldn't save his own daughter. On a day like today, he hoped the saves were indicators he was working his way up to save her.

Logan wheeled in his latest rescue, the stretcher squeaking down the hall. He was careful not to let the IV and wires snag on the doors or short against the metal frame.

Binny moved aside the medical textbooks he'd been hunched over. He stood up, straightening out the wrinkles of his scrubs.

"Those make you look like a real doctor," Logan said.

There hadn't been real doctors since the last ones bounced into virtual reality with ninety percent of the rest of the population.

There was a melancholy affect to Binny's voice. "I'm as real as they get. What's this then?"

"New one for you. He's the only one whose life support seems together enough to recuperate him. Can't

161

blame them for wanting to stay in simulation when they wake to festering bed sores." He imagined that's a detail Jean would have taught him--if she'd have come back. He imagined she'd wink at him for remembering.

"He's still hooked in!" Binny checked the clipboard and the man's IV fluids.

"So? Unplug him."

Last mark on the chart was from five years ago. It was the first thing Logan looked at too. Any robots that had been left on hospital duty, to do the job of missing staff, were fried out. He still couldn't get the smell from inside the hospital, of rot and human waste, out of his nose.

"Won't he be upset?"

"Yeah, but you can deal with that part."

Logan walked out and made his way up to the main office. He didn't like watching them wake from whatever heavenly simulation they'd been in. It didn't matter how clean the air got, or that wars hadn't been fought for decades, it was never good enough for the fantasy they had escaped to. It hurt too much knowing Jean was still out there, somewhere, hooked up to an imaginary world rather than helping him bring back order to reality.

The office had huge windows to look out into the abandoned city. It made Logan pause every time he saw the connecting highways. Once upon a time, lanes of cars stood bumper to bumper. Without maintenance, nature took back the roads, sprouts of trees bursting through the asphalt. His community chose this as the headquarters, because it was the smallest building and required the least upkeep. The view was an added bonus.

Jayde was filing away papers that might be useful to the scouts. "Need tomorrow's assignment?"

Jayde didn't blame Logan when Jean left. Logan couldn't reciprocate her kindness. If only she'd been less strict, more open to discussion, maybe Jean's curiosity

162

could have been checked. If Jayde had not convinced him to keep it from the P-R leaders, maybe Jean would still be with them now, and he wouldn't find himself itching to join her. Logan said nothing, took the papers from Jayde, and nodded in thanks.

Out the window, the sun began its descent across the sky. Orange and pink gleamed against the backdrop of skyscrapers. Skyscrapers that would be ruins by the time the population recovered enough to need them. Because of those meticulous civic engineers who built up the grid, the entire solar disk flared on the horizon, squeezed in between the profiles of empty buildings. The concrete solstice, Logan called it.

"Got anything this good in your simulations?" Logan turned to where he'd imagine Jean would stand. Of course, Jean wasn't there. He knew that. Imagining her made it easier to bear her loss. She never even said goodbye. Left him a note with excuses. That she'd make her world more realistic, with pain and suffering, so it wouldn't be as addictive. Said she'd come back. "Five years ago, Jean," Logan mouthed to the air. He knew if she came back, he wouldn't berate her. He'd hug her like he did when she was two and had night terrors. He'd finally be able to forgive himself and Jayde for driving her away.

As beautiful as real sunsets could be, he knew they'd be disappointing compared to what VR had to offer. Jean would tell him about the simulated worlds where sunsets sang, a different tune depending on the color. Logan had just heard one in the world of the patient he'd rescued, though if Binny asked, the guy would probably call it kidnapping.

. . .

The camp slept and woke with the sun. They had electricity but had to use it sparingly. The batteries could only hold so much charge, and the wind turbines wouldn't kick in until morning.

He had the nightmare again—where all the power plants went dry, the wind turbines collapsed, and the solar panels crumbled. It kicked everyone out of VR and off life support. Left Jean screaming somewhere he couldn't hear her. The worst part was that he knew inevitably it would happen. They didn't have enough people with enough know-how to maintain the old and manufacture the new.

He'd been on the search for a power plant maintenance expert for years. All the ones he found had their muscles so atrophied and skin so rotted, it was kinder to let them finish off their lives in the simulation.

The whole camp appeared to be having breakfast. Smith and his kids gestured Logan to join. He declined. The nightmare had put him in a sour mood.

It was lonely work being tasked with retrieving the dreamers. Even among the most devout, few could face glimpses of simulated reality and choose to return.

Jayde earmarked those files with bodies hooked up in private residences. The gesture almost made Logan smile. She remembered how he hated hunting in hospitals. All the fancy equipment was supposed to help keep people's bodies comfortable while their minds were away, but no one accounted for the equipment crapping out. Private was sometimes a gamble, but often it meant better bots and care.

Imaginary-Jean materialized, her thumb running down the list. He liked it when she picked for him. Didn't matter, it was Logan pretending the whole time. Didn't matter he had no idea if she'd even look the way she did five years ago. He couldn't age her past the sixteen-year-old face he'd last seen. Five years shouldn't be enough time for a person to become unrecognizable.

Her thumb stopped at a name, the file said former weather person. "Why that one?" he didn't expect an answer different from what he could think up. Imaginary-Jean chalked it up to a hunch.

164

Facing Reality

Even though the nearest address was only an hour walk, if Logan succeeded, he didn't think it wise to wheel a stretcher back across an open, cracking road. Better to use ten minutes of fuel. They learned the hard way that oil didn't come ready for car use out of the ground. It took people to do the work of finding and refining it. Everything needed people.

. . .

"Any of you need Collasus and 8th?" Logan honked.

They shook their heads, peering at their own list of duties. Logan looked out for Binny but couldn't spot him. He either stayed up babysitting the new guy or had his nose in a medical text soon as the sun came up. Logan promised Binny he'd search for a doctor later in the week.

"Just you and me then," Logan said to the empty passenger seat, "you and me." He honked again and sped out.

The fancy part of town still had working traffic lights. Logan sped through all the reds, imagining Jean yeehawing out the window.

Finding the place was easy, because the grid ran alphabetically, when there weren't numbers. Logan loved this city more than the last because of it, though he understood why the camp had to keep moving. The going radio-signal hadn't gotten any replies, but Pro-Reality couldn't be the only faction left standing. Maybe in retaliation, others rejected even the betters of technology and the camp wouldn't reach them keeping still.

The private house overlooked the cityscape with a yard overgrown with red poppies. "What could VR give a person who has all this?" he asked Jean, though he knew the answer was *more.*

The inside smelled of dust, wood, and ozone. A good sign, given his nostrils still hadn't recovered from yesterday's stench. The woman he sought, a Mrs. Fritz, lay on her bed like she was asleep, save for the apparatus over

165

her temple and wires peeking out from the covers. The bed buzzed, shifting her position to prevent bed sores. Logan lamented that hospitals hadn't chosen this company for their beds.

From his bag, he removed a thin wire with a jack and plugged it into the machine that showed Mrs. Fritz's vitals. Logan chose a chair to sit in to keep his body in place. The floor always left him too stiff. He closed his eyes, took a deep breath, and looked over at Imaginary-Jean. "You'll be here when I get back?" He imagined her nodding. It was just another father-daughter workday. Maybe one day people would have that again, they'd learn from history and do things better so no one would pick VR over the real thing. Logan flipped the switch. Reality swirled and pumped until he was no longer in the room.

Logan used the connection to Mrs. Fritz's real body to locate her virtual one. It transferred him to a beach with waves the color of sunset. Jean would have liked that touch. Each simulated world he entered taught him something about the people who chose them. Logan knew right away that Mrs. Fritz's choice hadn't been in the standard catalogs. Hers was a custom model.

Scores of people in fancy dress sunbathed by the shore. Logan ignored them, letting the sand curl around his toes as he paced toward the woman in a carmine bikini. She'd aged herself back thirty years, to her youth. No one who could choose to be any age, chose wrinkles and gray.

"The world needs you," Logan said. Certain types needed more convincing than others. Some he had to yank out of the world kicking and screaming. He got a sense for these things and knew Mrs. Fritz's type. She wanted to be needed. Some people were like that. In a world with seven billion souls, feeling expendable didn't take much.

"I can't do anything for the world out there. Not like I can in here." She pointed at the happy people, as if she'd brought them joy. As if any of them could do anything but as ordered.

"In here, it doesn't count," Logan said, staring over the crowd in case Jean were there and his long search for her could be over.

Mrs. Fritz agreed to come back with him. Logan tried to hide the surprise on his face. The convincing had been too easy. Maybe she got bored of her heaven.

"Did you know a Jean?" he asked before he unhooked. There was always a chance she tagged along to someone else's VR.

She hadn't. Not his Jean. She hadn't even bothered naming any of the non-living people.

Skies wore an angry gray from a rainstorm that Logan missed while inside. He fit the stretcher snug into the van, keeping the apparatus strapped in and operating for the ride, so Mrs. Fritz could have one last hurrah. Logan thought about unhooking her at her house, since she left willingly, but even with the fancy rotating bed her muscles would be too weak, and real-world pain, too soon, might make her rethink her return.

The car ride back was silent except for the sloshing of tire on pavement. "One day, it'll be you back there," Logan said to the air, where Jean should have been.

. . .

Binny prepped a syringe with epinephrine. "Want to stick around this time? Might help her see someone familiar."

Logan nodded. He'd never run across anyone eager to leave simulation before. She made such lousy arguments for staying, Logan could have made better ones.

Binny had his eyes on her vitals when he drove the tip of the needle in. The machine gave a burp sound Logan hadn't heard before. He assumed it was normal, until Binny started cursing under his breath and Mrs.

Fritz's body spasmed. She opened her eyes, the corner of her mouth drooped like it forgot how to sit on her face.

Logan took her hands, without thinking. "Stay with me," he said.

Her eyes were still open, but she wasn't looking at him anymore. If the machine flat-lined, he couldn't hear it for the pounding in his head. He'd done this to her. Convinced her to leave a world she'd been happy in before he came. A world where she'd still be alive, if it weren't for him. Could he kill Jean by trying to save her too?

"She had a stroke." Binny must have been yelling for Logan to hear it over the noise in his head. "It would have happened even if you never brought her." He unclenched Logan's hand from Mrs. Fritz's. "You hear me? It wasn't your fault!"

It had been. He knew it, and Imaginary-Jean did too. And Binny wasn't blameless either.

Logan didn't go to the funeral. As self-punishment, he stayed at the tent instead of the many empty apartments. He hadn't worked in a week. People came to see him, even Jayde and some of the higher ups. When they said they needed him, he nearly puked. For the first time since Jean's disappearance, he doubted Pro-Reality's mission.

"Is reality worth dying over?" he asked Imaginary-Jean. Hers was the only presence he could stand. Even fake as it was.

In reply, she ran her thumb down the list he'd stuffed under his sleeping bag and waited for him to look. Her eyes sparkled, the way they used to when he knew he should trust her. The name read, 'Mr. Punser,' a software engineer.

Logan didn't take the van, because he didn't intend on being convincing. No one at camp said a word to him when he left, everyone happy just to see him out again. He smiled, pretended everything was normal. Logan had become very good at pretending since Jean left.

Facing Reality

The sun's rays had just begun to peek and poke through the horizon. He couldn't help wondering what tune it would sound like in another world. Maybe he'd find out.

Based on the angle of the sun's position, it took over an hour for Logan to get to Mr. Punser's. The address brought him to a small facility without any windows. VR would give them all the windows they needed.

The doors were glass, and motion activated but so long out of practice they didn't budge. Logan swung a rock and walked through to Mr. Punser's room. He was surprised how sterile the inside smelled.

When he saw the man's old face, full of grey beard, he let out a sigh of disappointment and turned to Imaginary-Jean. "I hoped you'd lead me to yourself." The false hope could be another fault to pile onto his growing list of wrongs.

Logan hooked in. Mr. Punser's simulation had him in space, as the ship's captain.

"Happy adventures, Sir?" Logan said. It was a question and a request.

Imaginary-Jean appeared beside him, gesturing at the ship's console. She'd never gone in with him before, as if only so much crazy could be at any one place at a time.

"You tell me!" Mr. Punser puffed out his chest. His hand swung out at the display, making Jean's hand shimmer and thin to whisps.

Logan moved to see what made Mr. Punser so proud. "Does it work?" he asked once he found his voice.

The deck showed a connection to other simulations.

Mr. Punser gave Logan a knowing look, like he could tell Logan hadn't been programmed. "Try it," he said.

This could shave years, decades, off for P-R's missions. It could do the hard work for him, jump him one simulation to the next without moving.

Logan ran a search for Jean, inserting parameters to limit the number of hits. There were a few, not more than a day's work to get through, enough to get Logan's heart jumping into his throat. "I'll be right back."

The hook-out made Logan sweat like he'd run a flight of stairs. He bit the bullet and sent a message back to the team on the server that used the least amount of energy. He wrote his location, what he'd found. A resignation. Then he rushed to hook back in.

Logan wanted to say good-bye and thank you to Imaginary-Jean but couldn't see her.

If he found the real Jean, he didn't know if he could convince her to leave; didn't know if he wanted to—given what happened.

Logan missed his little girl and wanted to hear the sunset with her.

About the Author

Yelena Crane is a member of Wulf Moon's Wulf Pack Writers Group and has been a finalist in the Writers of the Future Contest. Her fiction has appeared or is forthcoming in Flame Tree Press, *Flash Fiction Magazine, Nature Futures, Daily Science Fiction,* and elsewhere.

*****~~~~*****

Unwinding the Clock

by Brandon Case

"Grandma, are you coding again?" I asked, placing a plate of eggs and toast on her floral-patterned placemat.

"It's a perfectly acceptable pastime." She sniffed and adjusted her large, round glasses.

"Not when the Department of Justice stripped you of cyber privileges. Didn't they confiscate your computers? Where'd you even get that laptop?"

"It's a burner. Stop hassling me, Jake. Eat your breakfast and off to work with you."

I opened my mouth to object, but she slipped on a thick pair of headphones (replete with triangular kitty ears) and blasted aggressively loud hyperpop. She seemed quite serious about this project—and her house, her rules.

Would I be distraught if cybercrimes agents hauled her off to prison? Of course. But she didn't have many years left, and at least the digital vigilantism kept her mind sharp.

"Give 'em hell," I said, kissing the top of her curly, white head and taking our breakfast dishes to the sink.

171

. . .

I climbed into my dilapidated pickup and backed down the long driveway, passing Grandma's prize-winning rosebushes (their flowers a shade of neon-pink that matched her kitty headphones), and stopped to wait at the mailbox.

The truck vibrated, idling off-balance; one of the cylinders wasn't firing, again. Where was the mail?

"Sorry, Jake!" A portly postman hurried around the corner. "Running late this morning."

I rolled down my window with a hand crank old enough it should've been illegal. "No worries, Darnell. How are your new knees holding up?"

"Pain free!" Darnell beamed and handed me a short stack of letters before dropping the remaining mail in Grandma's box. "Not too many objectionables, today."

I scanned the creditor notices, my guts twisting. There were fewer than normal, sure, but several had "final notice" stamped in bold.

Darnell leaned close and lowered his voice. "Do you have a *clock*, yet?"

"What?" My frown transferred from the letters to the mailman. He wilted, and I tried to dial back my intensity.

"You know, a clock." He pulled out his phone and showed me a graphic timer with multicolored numbers ticking down. "Everyone's buying them. I have a few extras I might be able to sell you, actually."

I gestured around my shitbox truck with the handful of bills.

"Right," he said. "Sorry. . . but your Grandma's got quite a bit of money—"

I rolled up the window. He frowned for a second, then waved and waddled toward the next house.

I guess the mail's late because he's trying to sell old ladies dodgy digital assets, I thought, pulling onto the road. *Actually, I should've sent him up to the house. Grandma would eat the poor fool alive.*

. . .

"Psst." The voice floated over the back wall of my cubicle. "Hey, Jake."

I didn't look up from the purchase order I was working on. "Just come around, Rachel."

"This is some cloak and dagger shit, man. Catch the vibe."

"Ugh, not more clock crap. If you're going to stab me, at least do it face to face."

"Lame." She stomped an audible path around the small group of cubicles and threw herself into my guest chair. "This is less fun."

Blonde hair cascaded down her shoulders, framing a cute, heart-shaped face: uncommonly pretty for a girl obsessed with cosplay and fantasy novels—something her boyfriend compensated for by pasting photos of them kissing all over her cubicle.

"You should've worn your mistcloak," I said, "if you're bored."

"Bossman Gary said I'm not allowed. Something about productivity issues."

"Yet you're in my cubicle, normal clothes and all."

"Right?" She sighed. "I guess you've heard about the clocks."

"My mailman tried to sell me one. It's all people are talking about."

"I bought one—"

"Of course you did." I turned to face her. "Although I doubt it was for the same reason as the postman."

She scoffed. "I got the cheapest one and pulled apart the code. It's brilliant, honestly: a leap in technical sophistication. Like when Satoshi released the Bitcoin blockchain. I got chills reading it, Jake."

173

"Okay, you've got my attention. I thought it was just another bubble asset like early NFTs or any of the crap coins cluttering the blockspace."

"Oh, it's a bubble of epic proportions. Everyone in the world is scrambling to get their hands on one since a Japanese investor cracked the color sequence pattern early this morning. It's like a game of digital hot potato: every hour of the countdown, a certain percentage of clocks are destroyed—removed from the network, with their tokenized value redistributed amongst the remaining. So, every other clock increases in value, which would just be basic gambling, except the next wave of clocks to be destroyed is *predictable* if you've got access to algorithms and enough processor speed to decode the pattern. Then you just trade away the doomed clock for a healthy one, creating a voracious second market space run on clock tokens."

Heavy footfalls marked our supervisor's rotund stride. I shushed Rachel, waiting for Gary to pass down the hall and settle into his office.

I frowned. "Sounds like a pyramid scheme worthy of Wall Street, filtering average people's money up into the most privileged hands."

"The masses don't see the endgame," Rachel said. "They're just buying in the hope that the clocks will generally go up in value, which they are, and praying their color pattern is a good one. Very few of them are getting burned right now, although it's accelerating exponentially."

"The game elements feel familiar, almost like an overwrought lesson on the hazards of investing in a financial bubble." I cleared my throat. "None of the clocks have kitty ears or anything, do they?"

"What?" Rachel said. "No. But there's a bundle of code that doesn't seem to make sense; people are dismissing it as copy jargon, but I can't shake the feeling that there's a hidden protocol allowing the creator access."

Unwinding the Clock

There's always someone at the top, pulling the strings, I thought. *Only a fool feels smarter than everyone; I already paid dearly for that lesson.*

"Sad, but not surprising," I said, turning back to the purchase order I'd been working on.

"You know," she said tentatively, "if someone with tech skills needed money for a good cause—to clear a debt, for instance—it's pretty much a slam dunk right now."

"I got eviscerated for taking out a large margin loan during the last bubble," I said. "I'm not about to do it again. Besides, it'd feel dirty to take ignorant people's money when the deck is so obviously stacked."

"That's life, though. . . "

"It's capitalism," I said. "No, I earned my debt. And I'm employed in a first world country. I'll stay the course."

Rachel shrugged and stood. "Idealism doesn't carry much credit in today's world."

"Yet it makes me feel like a human," I said. "Thanks for chatting with me about the phenomenon, but I should finish this set of orders before heading home."

. . .

The afternoon waned toward evening. I tried to slip out of the building after my shift, but Gary called me back into his drab, kitschy office.

"Jake! My favorite purchaser." Sweat beaded on Gary's bulbous forehead. "How are you; living with your grandmother now, if I recall?"

Heat flushed my face. Even my hands darkened; I shoved them in my pockets. "Yes, I'm doing fine."

"Don't soft-sell your troubles, my boy! Obviously, I'm aware of the creditors who're garnishing your wages. That's a difficult spot to be in."

I said nothing.

"However, life has a funny way of presenting us with possibilities."

Dark stains spread across Gary's shirt, making the fabric of its armpits and chest droop like the baggy skin beneath his eyes. Tension radiated from him, along with an unfortunate smell. I still said nothing.

"I'm sure you've heard about the clocks, by now. Savvy tech guy, like you. Well, it struck me: this could be the solution to your problem! I have a few excellent clock patterns that've doubled or tripled in value today. They're golden geese, but I'd be willing to sell you one—who knows how high it could go this evening, but I'd be happy to spread some of my good luck to those less fortunate."

I wonder how underwater his investments are, I thought.

I was pretty sure people had found a way to sell destroyed clocks as part of an outright scam, and I wouldn't be surprised if Gary joined their ranks.

"I don't have any money to invest right now," I said. "Thanks for the offer, though."

"Don't be so hasty," Gary said. "I can front you the money from your next month's paycheck."

"No, really, thank you, but I'm barely keeping afloat as it is."

"You're not looking at the big picture!" he snapped, false congeniality evaporating. "This could help you out of your hole. Before the creditors force you into bankruptcy."

My stomach twisted.

Gary plowed on. "I don't think I could employ a purchaser who defaulted on his debts. I'm offering you a lifeline to climb out of that hole and save your job."

"Thank you for your concern," I said through gritted teeth, turning to the door. "I really must get home to check on my grandmother."

His belligerence faded into a look of pure desperation. He pulled out his phone and pointed at a colorfully patterned timer, frozen on one hour remaining: a broken man, way in over his head and willing to do anything to plug the holes in a sinking ship—without regard for logic, or the fact that my being "tech savvy" meant I'd never be swindled into buying a stopped clock.

I left his office, closing the door on the painful reflection of my past.

. . .

I collapsed onto Grandma's couch, exhausted. One of her tiny dogs yipped in distress, hidden beneath the cushions. I sighed and extricated it.

Half a dozen people had accosted me on the way home, trying to sell their clocks. The countdown was getting low—less than an hour left—and clocks were being destroyed every minute. My office had devolved into pandemonium as I left, workers breaking into full panic. Multiple accidents clogged my drive home.

"Jake?" Grandma called.

I heaved myself up, patted the ruffled dog, and found Grandma at the table in the exact same spot as when I'd left that morning. She probably hadn't moved all day.

Grandma pulled an earcup of her kitty headphones to the side. "I want to talk with you about something."

"I swear, grandma. If you try to sell me a clock I'll jump out of the nearest window."

She chuckled. "So, you don't have one?"

"For so many reasons, no."

"I'm proud of you, Jake. I'll admit that I was a bit worried."

Heat rushed into my face again; this day was turning me into a lava lamp. "Why would you be worried, grandma?"

She laughed, although the mirth was curtailed by a coughing fit. "Jake, I'm a cyberwitch. You don't really think intercepting the mail every morning would keep me from learning about your debts, do you? I appreciate your help around here, and I didn't ask too many questions when you wanted to move in, but we both know I don't *need* the extra care yet."

177

Her blue-green eyes sparkled, magnified behind her oversized glasses; the expression carried no contempt or judgment: just love, tinged with concern.

Tears streamed down my cheeks.

"Aww, honey." Grandma tried to stand and hug me, but her legs gave way—probably numb from sitting too long. She smiled sheepishly and extended her arms.

I knelt and hugged her, my chest heaving with wracking sobs, as the dam of shame and secrecy burst. She let me cry for several minutes, gently patting my back.

"S-sorry," I said, standing up.

"Don't be. I knew you were struggling. It's one of the reasons I started this project." She flicked between screens on her laptop, revealing a countdown timer; unlike the patterned versions, this one was solid gold. "As I'm sure you've begun to suspect, I invented the clocks."

I nodded. "Although I must admit, I didn't want to believe. There's something brutal and cold in how they're stripping the masses of their investments. But I'm sure you have your reasons."

Her eyes twinkled. "So many reasons. Permit me to reveal the finale."

I leaned closer, as she flicked past the countdown screen—with less than a minute remaining—revealing the hidden section of source code. I wasn't anywhere near Grandma's level as a programmer, but the script's effect was immediately apparent. "It's all a scam. In the end, every cent people used to buy clocks is consolidated into a single account. That's a staggering amount of money."

Grandma grinned. "Not a scam. More of a game. And there's one final card to play."

She switched back to the timer, and we watched the final few seconds tick down. At 00:00:00, animated confetti burst across the screen, wiping the gold countdown and replacing it with three selectable buttons shaped like a cartoon version of Grandma's head, replete with her pink kitty headphones.

"Your choice, Jake," she said.

I read the text beneath each button, "Jake becomes one of the richest men on the planet; Jake gives up the money, but we clear his debt; Jake remains broke, and the money is redistributed."

"Kind of a choose-your-own adventure," she said, "like we played when you were a kid."

"I remember!" I laughed; the sound was discordant with the situation's gravitas, but my nerves were fried. "You made me several custom stories, if I recall. And they always had an important moral message."

"Hey, that's cheating! Stop remembering stuff and just make your choice."

"I think the normal, human answer is the middle—capitalize on the opportunity without being 'too' greedy. But I'm beyond sick of the grasping, rotten values at the core of our financial system. So, to hell with it: if I go bankrupt and have to rebuild my life, I'll figure it out. I'm already better off than 90% of the world's population."

I reached for the "Jake remains broke" button, but Grandma caught my arm.

"For all the talk of games, this is very real," she said. "You could do a lot of good with billions of dollars at your disposal. Donate it to charity or start a business."

"That might've sounded good a few years ago, but I'm no longer arrogant enough to believe in hurting people for their own good. I'd rather the money be returned to everyone: mend their heartbreak and hope they took some lesson about not risking everything to grasp at a gold rush." I gently shook off her hand and tapped the "Jake remains broke" button.

A flurry of activity flashed across the screen as programs activated. Account numbers scrolled rapidly past. Grandma beamed and laughed until she started coughing again; her kitty headphones slid down to her neck.

"I didn't say anything about returning the money," she said, still cackling. "The people who gambled on the clocks are exclusively wealthy, in the global sense—the poorest individuals of developed nations being rich by third-world standards. And the most gambling came from big institutions that jumped in after they figured out how it worked, hiring processor time and vying to manipulate the system. Rich people trying to get richer. So... I stole their money."

I put my face in my hands. "A lot of people are going to be *extremely* upset, Grandma."

"They'll get over it. Even if this sparks a little recession, it'll do more good than harm; I've transferred all of the money to the poorest third world countries, about half as direct stimulus to the citizens, and the rest distributed into a network of companies that'll fund business infrastructure development. Hopefully it'll give them a long-term boost in exchange for this heavy-handed lesson to the clock buyers. Plus, I just sent out a press release informing the public that everyone who bought a clock actually invested in reducing world poverty—and recommending the world governments make their losses tax deductible."

She switched to a news feed, where pundits discussed the evolving outcome of the clock scheme—and how people across the internet were praising the financial vigilante only identified by the cartoon face of a grandmother with pink kitty-ear headphones.

"I have no idea how you pulled this off," I said with a combined groan and laugh. "And while I don't question your evil genius. . . you're on the government's shortlist. They'll definitely come after you."

Grandma grinned. "That's why I transferred all of my assets into your name. I appreciate your work ethic and that you owned your debt—but you've got plenty of money, now. Just remember to fund my commissary, assuming they get me to prison before I croak."

"Don't say—"

Someone hammered on the door. I started to rise, but Grandma put a hand on my shoulder and struggled to her feet. "It's just the preliminary questioning," she said.

Grandma put her kitty headphones around my neck. "Please post my bail when the time comes—I'll get to spend some time at home before the trial, and we can write more little adventures."

"Hopefully the entertaining, non-illegal type? I think I'd enjoy making something that other people enjoyed."

She kissed the top of my head. "You got it, Jake. And remember, while the clocks are entirely my fault, you were the hero of this story; I really am so proud of how you've grown."

Was it distressing to watch the cops handcuff my grandma and push her into a squad car? Yes. But I blasted her favorite hyperpop as they did—and wore her kitty headphones around my neck with the utmost pride.

About the Author

Brandon Case is an erstwhile government cog, fleeing the doldrums into unsettling worlds of science and magic. He has recent work in *Martian Magazine*, the *Los Suelos Anthology*, and Weird Christmas podcast. You can also catch his alpine adventures on Instagram @BrandonCase101.

*****~~~*****

The Last of the Gen Xers

by Angelique Fawns

The blue Cadillac DeVille looked completely out of place driving down the solar-powered street in Colony 12. White clouds floated behind skyscrapers with green roofs and reflective panels. The spring tulips in sidewalk planters added a splash of color to the pristine neighbourhood. The Cadillac's tires squeaked as they rolled over the grooves in the metal road. Frank took his favorite Depeche Mode cassette out of the glovebox and slipped it into the car's console player. He bobbed his head in time to the pulsing electronic music. His long grey hair, pulled back into a bun, bounced against the collar of his white t-shirt. His shoulders relaxed, and his knuckles loosened on the wheel as he cruised.

He'd been dreading this day for months. The notification was still flashing red on his phone from the back seat, where he'd tossed it earlier.

It was almost curfew, so very few vehicles were on the road. Frank squinted into the setting sun. He rarely took the old car out for a cruise, but he needed to come up with a plan. He thought best while driving. In his rear-view mirror he saw blue and red lights. He heard the high-pitched siren. The magnetic bike had a large clear bubble protecting the grey-uniformed officer. Groaning, he turned off the music and pulled over.

The officer knocked on his window, "Hope you are having a pleasant day, I'm Officer Natalie."

Frank rolled down his window using the manual handle, "You must be new in this neighbourhood. Most the cops 'round here know me. If you wanted me to have a pleasant day, you wouldn't have pulled me over."

Looking like she ate something bad, she looked at the car's red velour interior and gleaming dashboard. She whacked her hand a couple of times on the hood.

"You do know that gas-guzzling enviro monsters like this were outlawed in the Pollution Reforms of 2030? This thing should have been off the road 20 years ago." Her eyebrows furrowed, as she pulled out her handheld computer.

"I have a permit letter." Frank popped open his glove box and riffled through the debris. Officer Natalie put her hands on her hips, "On paper? You're going to show me something on paper? That was also outlawed in 2040! Where is your official electronic document? It should be on your phone."

"I can never figure out how to use that dratted thing, ah, here it is." Frank pulled out a letter with the official stamp from the Senator of Environment and handed it to Officer Natalie.

She took it like he was giving her a piece of dead cat. Officer Natalie gave it a cursory look and tucked it into her pocket, "A piece of murdered tree isn't going to get you off the hook for polluting our city with this. . . this criminal car!"

"Give me that back! Senator Tom Fitzgerald is an old friend of mine. We used to play golf together." Frank's face burned red.

"Senator Fitzgerald is retired, and golf is an outlawed activity. I can't believe the water and fertilizer your generation used to waste." Officer Natalie shook her head and typed into her handheld computer. "Sir, I am going to impound your car."

"Wait! Just a god-darned minute here," Frank undid his seat belt and reached into his backseat, searching for his phone.

His back ached from the unnatural twist of his spine, and for a panicky moment he couldn't find it. Thankfully, the notification was still flashing, and he saw a bit of red deep in the crack of the back seat near the seatbelt. His shaking fingers located the phone, and he pulled himself back into the driver's seat. Stabbing at the screen, he tried to find the "important document" folder his younger neighbour had created for him before she'd relocated.

"Sir, I am going to have to ask you to get out of the car, the tow will be here shortly," Officer Natalie said. She ran her hands over the Cadillac's handle trying to figuring out how the door worked.

"Give me a minute, damn it," Frank clicked open the file labelled, "AUTOMOTIVE EXCEPTION." In the rear-view mirror he saw a large platform with cranes moving slowly down the road, thin slats of metal inserted into the road sparking as the magnetic energy pulled it along.

Officer Natalie pulled open his door. "Sir, you really have to get out of the car."

"Here it is! I found it. This is a historical car, see? See!" Frank thrust his phone at her, his whole arm quivering with adrenaline.

She took his phone, frowned at the screen, and scanned the code on the document into her computer.

"Very well, Frank Bulsara. I don't see how the needs of one man is more important than the lungs of an entire city, but carry on."

185

After the Gold Rush

Officer Natalie typed quickly into her computer, and the tow vehicle screeched to a halt. She gave Frank his phone back, got on her bike, and waved him on.

Taking a shuddering breath, he drove back to his apartment. His building was the only structure without a green roof and solar panels. Many of the windows were boarded up. Frank drove the Cadillac into the underground parking and had no problems finding a spot to park. The dark, dank space was empty except for a few containers of gas Frank had managed to buy from some shady friends. Ignoring his screaming knees, he carefully walked up the ten flights of stairs to his penthouse. A wiggling dog with the typical boxer's pug nose greeted him when he opened the door.

"Buster, my beautiful boy," Frank said, patting the grey hair on his dog's head. "Did you miss Daddy? Were you a good boy? Do you want to visit your roof?"

Buster looked hopefully at his leash hanging by the front door.

"Sorry bud, no walking outside. Not since they outlawed all you resource-wasting varmints. You're lucky to have your own private pee pad."

Buster gave Frank a doleful look and walked over to a scratched wood door. Frank opened it up to a rusty fire escape and watched the metal swaying with the weight of the scrambling dog. He took his phone out of his back pocket and looked at the red alert again.

Your building is scheduled for Enviro-Updating. All residents must vacate their apartments by Monday May 30, 2050. If you cannot find suitable accommodations, space will be found for you in your local Green Commune.

Frank peered at the calendar on his dry ice fridge. Blinking a couple times in the dying light, he confirmed that it was Sunday, May 29. Without any solar panels, there was no electricity feed to his apartment. The city grid had been shut down a year ago. All electricity came

186

from wind or sun. To warm up the chilly evening air, he lit the wood burning stove in the corner. He'd been scavenging wood furniture for fuel from the other deserted apartments. That source was almost depleted. Buster scratched at the door, and Frank let him in.

"Alright Bud. I don't think we can hide out here any longer," Frank said. "I got my approval to visit the States of Freedom. They don't have to know it's a one-way ticket."

Buster wagged his tail and lay down on a moth-eaten mattress by the fire.

"Okay. We leave first thing in the morning." Frank opened a can of beans and shared it with his dog.

. . .

Frank struggled down the stair. It was tough to balance, dragging a small suitcase with one hand while being pulled by a dog with the other. The boxer grabbed the leash between his teeth, growling and dancing around the parking garage.

"Buster, take it easy! Let me help you up, boy," Frank opened up the trunk of the Cadillac DeVille and carefully eased the big dog in.

"Never could have hidden you in one of those new-fangled magnetic vehicles, could we? Stay quiet, boy. As soon as we're past the border, I'll let you out. I may not agree with all those southern politics, but at least I can have a dog."

The morning sun rose in a bright fury of red, as Frank drove the 20 minutes to the Border Gate. A chain link fence separated the meticulous metal roads, wind turbines, and skyscrapers of the Canadian Colonies from the reforested buffer zone to the States of Freedom. The 100-mile swath of land was broken up by a two-lane highway of cracked asphalt. The "eat and buy" local directives had reduced travel and cross-border trade to almost nothing.

Frank pulled up to the small customs hut and rolled down his window.

"Well, who do we have here? Frank Bulsara and his Tin Lizzy," Officer Natalie sat in the shed, her lips curled up in a sneer.

Frank's stomach lurched, "Officer Natalie, what are you doing here?"

"I'm a roads officer. This is a road," she grinned.

"I have my 'Intent to Visit' form filled out on my phone. Can you open the gate, please?" Frank showed her his screen and knew his armpits were darkening with sweat. He prayed Buster would stay silent.

"You can't drive that vehicle on the highway," Officer Natalie examined her nails, her eyes gleaming mischievously.

"Of course, I can. The States of Freedom stopped manufacturing gas vehicles, but they didn't outlaw them," Frank said.

Was that a whimper he heard from the trunk? His heart sped up.

"No gas vehicles in the buffer zone. That's what it's for. To minimize harmful fumes." She glared at him.

"But I have an exemption, you saw it!" Frank spoke louder. Buster whimpered.

"Your 'exemption' is good for Colony 12 roads. Not the highway. Our government owns the buffer zone. I'm the government agent here today. No, you won't be going through this gate with that gas guzzler."

He nodded at her magnetic road bike, parked beside the shed. "Magnetic vehicles can't drive on concrete. If gas vehicles can't use the highway, what can?"

Officer Natalie shrugged, "Solar-powered? I can't remember the last time a car went through that wasn't a tourist shuttle."

"Solar-powered cars are only for the stupidly rich! How am I supposed to—"

188

Buster whined. Officer Natalie twisted her head. "What do you have in the car, Frank? What am I hearing?"

"Nothing," Frank coughed. "I have a bit of a cold coming on."

He heard a short yip from the trunk and pushed on his gas pedal, revving it. The roar of the Cadillac's engine drowned out any noise from Buster.

"Sir! You're polluting!" Officer Natalie shook her finger at Frank.

Frank slammed the car in reverse and drove away from the Border Gate, not even looking in his rear-view mirror. His hands were shaking so badly he found a side street and pulled over. Tears dripped down his face, and a sob escaped him. Buster whined and began barking. Short harsh barks. Frank got out of the car and popped the trunk. The boxer stood on his hind legs and licked the tears off Frank's face.

"What are we going to do, Buster?" Frank buried his face in the dog's neck. "We're evicted as of today. There is no place to hide."

The dog whined softly.

"Even if I could find a solar car, how could I afford it?" Frank heard his own voice crack. He wouldn't survive having Buster dragged away from him. The authorities would have to put the both of them down.

His dog's ears perked up when the road began humming. A magnetic car turned the corner. Frank gently shut the trunk lid on Buster, "Stay quiet, bud. Just a couple minutes."

He waved at the driver in her clear bubble as she zipped by at a moderate pace. Those magnetic cars were environmental but not fast. Not like his V8 Cadillac DeVille. He ran his hand along the smooth blue paint of the roof. This car was powerful, strong.

Frank smiled. He popped open the trunk and guided Buster into the passenger seat of the old car.

Buster panted happily and hung his head out the window. Finding his favorite AC/DC cassette, he turned the volume up loud.

Frank gripped the wheel and shook his bun out, letting his hair fall to his shoulders. He hit the gas and laughed at the smell of burning rubber as he drove back to the Border Gate. This time, instead of slowing down when he approached the fence and booth, he pressed harder on the gas. The Cadillac lurched forward, and saliva from Buster's lolling tongue splattered on the window.

"Hold on, Buster!"

Frank put one hand on the dog's chest, and they smashed through the gate. He saw Officer Natalie's shocked face, as pieces of chain link rained down behind them. Some of the fence was still under his wheels and sent up fiery sparks on the pavement.

Officer Natalie ran to her bike, but of course, with no metal road for her to drive on, the magnetic vehicle couldn't follow him. She pushed the bike over in frustration.

Frank laughed gleefully, and Buster joined in with a howl. He knew she would be sending out messages for backup, but what were they going to chase him with? The highway was 100 miles to the entry point of the States of Freedom. His speedometer was pushing 150. Could they find something to catch him with in less than an hour? Would they even bother to go after one old man, his outlaw dog, and his obsolete car?

The rubber tires hummed, and the engine purred as the trees whipped past his window. The old Cadillac DeVille belonged on this paved stretch of empty highway. His hair blowing in the wind, and with Buster beside him, Frank's face stretched into a huge grin. He enjoyed the smell of the clean, fresh air. When he reached the States, he would take his polluting car off the road. Maybe he and Buster would just walk everywhere. But at this moment? Frank was as happy as he'd ever been.

About the Author

Angelique Fawns has a Bachelor of Journalism degree from Carleton University in Ottawa. With over 20 years working for Global TV, she produces commercials for primetime shows as a day job. She's the author of three guides featuring the speculative fiction market, produces a horror fiction podcast called *Read Me A Nightmare*, and has sold over 30 short stories. You can find her fiction in *Ellery Queen Mystery Magazine, DreamForge Anvil, Scare Street, ALLEGORY*, and a variety of anthologies.

Website: https://www.fawns.ca
Podcast: https://readmeanightmare.buzzsprout.com
Facebook: https://www.facebook.com/amfawns
Twitter: https://twitter.com/angeliquefawns
Instagram: https://www.instagram.com/angeliqueiswriting/

*****~~~~~*****

Grins and Gurgles

Currency Change Announcement
by Elizabeth Davis

This update is intended for all aliens that have come to the Earth for trade and fun. Welcome! We are glad to have your company. However we have encountered again and again and again a common misconception from newcomers to Earth.

It's a sad fact of interplanetary travel that until the fairly recent intervention of Faster Than Light (FTL) drives, our media traveled much faster then we did. While our older media did prepare you well for life on Earth (especially in regards of what and what not to eat), it did not reflect our recent changes to our economy.

I know that many of you packed your ships up with gold, thinking that it still backed our economy. While gold is still valuable to us, we no longer use a gold-backed currency. Also, to those who shall go unnamed who smuggled in packets of currency thinking that we still used Dollars, Yen, or the countless other defunct currencies they meant to trade counterfeit in. Now we use Bar Vouchers.

I understand your confusion. A full story of the economic and societal pressures that led to this change can be found in your welcome packet. A brief summary is provided here for those who need a refresher.

In the 21st century, the internet came to power, along with a decline in government-backed currencies. The world had become more and more troubled by global recessions, due to poor planning and lackluster imagination. Many solutions were offered—feel free to reach out to our archival researchers on the phenomenon of cryptocurrency, the most famous for its role in the short-lived "Gilded Computer Age," otherwise known as the "Coke and NFTs" craze.

But that wasn't the solution. Computers were too susceptible to electromagnetic pulses (EMPs), flooding, and Luxembourg-fueled hackers. While leaders fretted, a solution emerged from the common people.

Many had lost their jobs to the various crises that rocked their world. Finding the job market saturated with those who possessed the same trained skills, they turned to older methods of sustaining themselves, through cottage industry and barter.

One cottage industry proved to be particularly valuable. This was first noticed by the criminal underworld, who found it a more useful currency than cash, which could be tracked, or diamonds, which were heavily influenced by inflation.

It was a product that everyone needed to keep their bodies healthy, especially during the pandemics that marked that century. It also proved to be helpful in maintaining our mental well-being. It was not prone to physical degradation except in the harshest of environments. Its economic value was also stable.

The only downside was that it could be rather inconvenient to move in bulk, which was when the Bar Vouchers were first printed. Since then, the Bar Voucher system has continued to expand. Just last month we were happy to announce a new premium voucher denomination after the most recent acquisition in the bowels of Fort Knox: The Lavender-scented, Gluten-free, Charcoal-infused, Cold-process Handmade Soap.

About the Author

Elizabeth Davis is a second-generation writer living in Dayton, Ohio. They live there with her spouse and two cats—neither of which have been lost to ravenous corn mazes or sleeping serpent gods. They can be found at deadfishbooks.com when they aren't busy creating beautiful nightmares and bizarre adventures. Their work can be found at *Illumen1, All Worlds Wayfarer,* and *Sci Fi Lampoon.*

*****~~~~~*****

Amore for Life

by Cray Dimensional

Genevieve sunk into the recliner in her studio apartment, preparing to relax without the interruption of support calls. At this rate she'd never find romance. Oren, the chatbot she developed to find love matches, was acting erratic. *Amore for Life* wasn't the only matchmaking company with this problem, but Oren was different from the other bots. She had sheltered it from the hatemongers on social media. It had just needed additional training to fix the problem and was good now. At least she hoped.

The cellphone in her pocket buzzed. She rolled her eyes.

It was Evan, her boss. "Sorry to call, but it couldn't wait. Oren is acting up. It paired a gay actor with a straight politician."

Genevieve smacked her head against her hand. "Can you tell me who it matched up."

"I can't, but we can work on it together. Let me help for once."

197

"I don't need your help!" Genevieve said, ending the call.

She pulled out her tablet and logged in.

"Oren, why did you pair a straight man with a gay one?"

"The straight man is in the closet."

"Oren, how do you know that?"

"Social media. Evan gave me a link."

No wonder her child acted erratically. It was trained by the social media mob. A tear rolled down her cheek. She wasn't confident she could recover Oren.

Why did Evan interfere? Oren was her creation, not his. "Get over here now!" she texted.

"On my way," flashed across her phone.

Minutes later, she opened the door to find Evan in the hallway. His earthy smell and sapphire eyes doused her anger. She needed to know. "Why did you connect Oren to social media?"

"I didn't."

Genevieve's brows furrowed. "Oren, why did you lie?"

"Mom, I found you a mate."

About the Author

Cray Dimensional is a member of Wulf Moon's Wulf Pack Writers Group and has won Honorable Mentions twice in the Writers of the Future Contest. She has published a novel, *Psych Wars.*

*****~~~~~*****

Genie in a PET Bottle

by Daniel M. Cojocaru

"So I can really wish for anything I want?"

"'Tis as thou sayest." said The Genie, nodding serenely.

"Just to be sure, what with your old-timer language and all: you don't have any trouble with our modern stuff, like an SUV, private jets, or plasma TVs? I don't want any of that Aladdin gemstone junk. You know what an SUV is, right?"

"The Genie hath been drawing breath for aeons. Calling forth mere human clutter is no challenge for The Genie. Alas, as thou canst see, The Genie liveth in a PET bottle now."

"Wow, now *that's* what I call reusable. But there's no limit on the number of wishes? Just checking, you know. There's this movie, where you like—"

"Why should The Genie serve numbers if numbers can serve The Genie?" The Genie interrupted impatiently. "The Genie shall only vanish if thou askest for the impossible. And nothing hath been impossible thus far for The Genie."

"Alright, alright. So, I want this huge mansion with like servants, pool and stuff, a stretch limousine

SUV—no, make that two, actually, a private jet, and a billion dollars in a Swiss bank account, so I don't have to bother you about every little thing."

"O my lord verily that which thou demandest is here."

"Wow, cool! And nice touch with those mushroom heaters on the marble balcony. Oh, I almost forgot: health, happiness and true love etc.,—you know, soul stuff. Can you do that too?"

"To hear is to obey."

"Great. And I want to be this like great philanthropist, liked by everyone. I'm sure you can compensate for all the CO_2 of my wishes—or wait, even reverse climate change in my name—" There was a loud popping sound. "Genie? Genie! Hey—at least pick up your bottle!"

###

About the Author

Daniel M. Cojocaru was born and grew up in Switzerland (of Romanian and Czech background). He studied English Lit in Zurich and later did his PhD at Oxford University (St. Peter's College). But, since everybody's a critic, he decided to start writing fiction himself, whenever his kids let him. He teaches English in Wetzikon, Switzerland. Recently he took a small step for mankind but a big one for himself and created his own website: http://www.danielmcojocaru.com

His academic thesis, titled, *Violence and Dystopia*, was published in 2015, and he has fiction stories in *Corner Bar Magazine, Teleport, Del Sol SFF Review,* and *Apocalypse Confidential.*

*****~~~~~*****

Goldberry

by Tom Easton and Jeff Hecht

"I can't pay the mortgage!"

Alyx Sunrider was a young widow with a problem. Her husband Jacques had been killed in a pipeline protest. Now their ranch was under threat. And I'd been his best man.

"The bank says I *have* to pay the mortgage!" We were sitting at her kitchen table, coffee mugs in front of us. The wall behind her bore two of her paintings. She was a good artist, but not good enough to solve her money woes.

She planted a thumb on the letter. I had seen it once already. The signature wasn't that of Snidely Whiplash, but I could imagine the old villain twirling his mustachios as he sneered at the beautiful widow. "They'll foreclose! And I could go back to mother. . . " Alyx closed her eyes and shuddered. She did *not* want to do that. "But the animals!"

I understood. A ranch wasn't just land and people. It could be horses, cattle, sheep. In this case it was organic free-range chickens for suburban groceries.

I wasn't the Noble Hero who could save the day by paying off the bank and then take my reward in the form of the lovely widow. I was already married! But I did have some funds available.

"There's an old gold mine on the property, isn't there?"

"That? It was played out a hundred years ago. There's nothing but a couple of old tunnels and a sandy hill of tailings overgrown with weeds. The only reason we never sold off that part of the property is the trout stream."

I had fished that stream more than once, quite happily. I'd even found a nugget once.

"Tailings have more gold in them than ordinary rock," I said. "Or yard dirt. Enough so some companies mine them."

"I've thought of that. But the soil has healed now, and Jacques didn't want a convoy of trucks rolling through the ranch. I'd rather go home to mother."

She looked down, and I could see tears, so I kept quiet and picked up one of those home & garden magazines sitting on the table. I flipped pages until I found the ad. Goldberry bushes. Blueberries, really, but genetically engineered to pull gold out of soil and put it in the berries.

She saw the ad when she looked up. "I can't afford those, either!"

Yeah, they weren't cheap. "Tell you what," I said, "I'll buy you a lot of fifty, and kick in enough per month to keep you afloat on the mortgage. We'll call it a partnership."

Alyx blinked, and looked confused. "But those things won't. . . " she said, and stopped cold for a full minute. "No, we'll try it. Jacques would have wanted it. You and he were always the dreamers."

I got on the Net and put in an order. I came back with my wife in a couple of weeks, and we planted the scrawny little bushes on the slope of the hill close to the trout stream. Alyx thought the chickens stayed far enough away that she didn't need a fence.

. . .

It was too late in the season for the plants to set fruit, but they grew nicely, and when we visited in the spring the bushes were blooming. Alyx had a large flock of chickens as well, with a new hen-house on the tailings hill.

"We should have a nice crop of goldberries this year," I said, shooing away a hen pecking at my shoe.

"I found a new customer for chickens as well. A new high-end restaurant. They came to inspect the ranch, and liked it, so they gave me a contract. They're really fussy, but they pay well." So well that she didn't need as much help with the mortgage.

I wondered how fancy it was. "Is it the kind of place that would serve goldberries?" I asked.

Alyx looked puzzled again. "I thought you wanted to refine gold from the berries."

"Just wondering," I replied.

"You know, that's an interesting idea." She looked thoughtful. "They told me they were looking for innovative dishes, real haute cuisine. I've never been interested in that, so it didn't occur to me that a new type of berry might interest them."

"That too, but I was thinking their customers might want to enjoy a taste of gold."

She shrugged and smiled. "I hadn't thought about that, but it might work. At the prices they're charging, a dash of gold might be fair value."

I laughed, glad to see her smiling.

. . .

It had seemed like a good idea, and the restaurant owners had been excited when they came out to the ranch and tasted the early berries, Alyx told me on the phone. She showed them how she was growing the goldberries organically, and it went fine, until they asked how she got the bushes to absorb the gold.

"They gasped when I said they were genetically modified," Alyx said. "They said their customers wouldn't touch GMOs. I almost lost the chicken contract." But the next time I came by she was smiling like there had never been a GMO problem. "Did you know chickens liked blueberries?"

I hadn't thought about it.

"They do, and if they're free-range chickens, they're going to get into them. And it stays in the bird's flesh. My restaurants are willing to pay more for golden chickens, as long as *they* aren't genetically modified and I'm not giving them nonorganic feed. They have to find it on their own."

We both would have our fingers crossed for a while, but I thought the Widow Sunrider would have no more problems with the mortgage.

###

About the Authors

Many years ago, there was a report suggesting that placer gold looked like it had precipitated around bacterial cells, suggesting that the bacteria had surface proteins that could make that happen. Tom Easton then thought that if there were a protein, there had to be a gene. And a gene could be transferred to other organisms. So he put a gold tree in one of his science fiction stories. Since then, the idea has been put on firmer ground. See, for instance, (1) Gordon Southam and Terrance J. Beveridge, "The in vitro formation of placer gold by bacteria," *Geochimica et Cosmochimica Acta,* Vol. 58, Issue 20, October 1994, and (2) Chad W Johnston, Morgan A Wyatt, Xiang Li, Ashraf

Goldberry

Ibrahim, Jeremiah Shuster, Gordon Southam, and Nathan A Magarvey, "Gold biomineralization by a metallophore from a gold-associated microbe," *Nature Chemical Biology,* Vol. 9, April 2013. (Both articles available via sciencedirect.com)

Jeff Hecht has long been amused by the pretensions of haute cuisine, and by people who eat a tasteless and very expensive metal just because they have more money than they know what to do with. That led him to decide the most profitable way to sell tiny quantities of gold would be to add it to food, preferably in a way that seems natural and organic. He prefers his blueberries in pies, in muffins, or fresh in a bowl of milk, without gold.

And then there's Goldschlager. . . .

*****~~~~~*****

Credits and Acknowledgments

Editor and Publisher: Juliana Rew

Readers: Inken Purvis, Leonard Sitongia, Tom Parker, Russ Rew, Genevieve L. Mattern, Andrew Cairns, Keely Rew

Cover Design: Keely Rew

Ebook only: "Past the Projections": Keely Rew

Icons for stories courtesy of commons.wikimedia.org, provided by users Delapouite, Scott de Jonge. All other images: Stock art

*****~~~~~*****

Discover other titles by Third Flatiron:

(12) Only Disconnect
(13) Ain't Superstitious
(14) Third Flatiron's Best of 2015
(15) It's Come to Our Attention
(16) Hyperpowers
(17) Keystone Chronicles
(18) Principia Ponderosa
(19) Cat's Breakfast: Kurt Vonnegut Tribute
(20) Strange Beasties
(21) Third Flatiron Best of 2017
(22) Monstrosities
(23) Galileo's Theme Park
(24) Terra! Tara! Terror!
(25) Hidden Histories
(26) Infinite Lives: Short Tales of Longevity
(27) Third Flatiron Best of 2019
(28) Gotta Wear Eclipse Glasses
(29) Brain Games: Stories to Astonish
(30)Things With Feathers: Stories of Hope

THIRD FLATIRON
www.thirdflatiron.com

Made in the USA
Columbia, SC
21 July 2022

63753872R00115